MARVEL

MONSTERS UNLEASHED!

BEWARE THE GLOP!

Written by
STEVE BEHLING

Autumn
Publishing

Autumn
Publishing

Published in 2018
by Autumn Publishing
Cottage Farm
Sywell
NN6 0BJ
www.igloobooks.com

Written by Steve Behling
Cover illustration by Skan Srisuwan

CLA006 0718
2 4 6 8 10 9 7 5 3 1
ISBN 978-1-78905-401-9

Printed and manufactured in UK

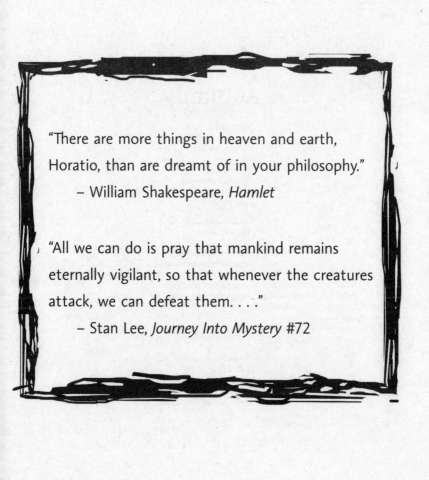

"There are more things in heaven and earth, Horatio, than are dreamt of in your philosophy."
– William Shakespeare, *Hamlet*

"All we can do is pray that mankind remains eternally vigilant, so that whenever the creatures attack, we can defeat them. . . ."
– Stan Lee, *Journey Into Mystery* #72

PROLOGUE

HAVE YOU EVER tried to smash a big blob of goo with your fist?

No?

Of course you haven't. Why would you? It's a silly question. You have better things to do, like play video games or read comic books.

But the Hulk couldn't say the same thing. Because right at that moment, he quite literally had nothing better to do – nothing else he *could* do – than to smash a big green gamma-powered fist into a gigantic, oozing mess of goo.

"Hulk smash!" thundered the jade giant. His balled-up hand went flying into a wall of wet glop.

1

It made the Hulk mad, this goo or whatever it was. It was alive, somehow. It seemed to think. It kept coming after the Hulk. It wanted to hurt him.

Why couldn't the stupid goo just leave Hulk alone?

He had been fighting like this for, what, hours now? Maybe longer than that. The battle began in a remote California desert, where Bruce Banner had been working on an important renewable energy project for S.H.I.E.L.D. During a test, something strange had happened: something attacked the laboratory. What it was, exactly, Banner couldn't say – he had never seen anything like it before.

Given time, Banner could have studied it, found out exactly what the thing was. But all the excitement caused his pulse to race.

His heart beat faster and faster.

In a matter of seconds, Banner underwent a startling transformation.

Where once stood a mild-mannered scientist, there now stood a seven-foot-tall green man-monster that the world called the Hulk.

As the Hulk roared, he slammed another impossibly huge fist into the mysterious goo that had suddenly disrupted Banner's experiment. The substance flew apart where the Hulk hit it, and little clumps of it flew all around him. The Hulk snarled, turned, and saw the various bits of goo slowly flow back to each other, coalescing as a whole.

What *was* this stuff?

Whatever it was, the goo reared upward, and somehow towered over the towering Hulk. It seemed to move with a mind all its own. Like a tidal wave, it flowed toward the Hulk, enveloping him completely!

If you were there in the desert at that precise moment, you would have heard the Hulk's roar, muffled through the thick layers of glop. The substance stretched over and around the Hulk, and started to squeeze his body all over. It constricted his rib cage. No matter how the Hulk expanded his chest, the goo kept on getting tighter and tighter. No matter how the Hulk clawed at the substance with his fingers, the goo clung to his skin.

The Hulk wasn't big on realizing things while he was in the middle of a fight. But something started to dawn on him.

He couldn't breathe. He could survive for a while without oxygen. He was the Hulk, after all. With his gamma-powered lungs, he could survive underwater or even in the vacuum of space.

But only for a while.

This made him angry.

And the madder the Hulk gets, the stronger he gets.

The green behemoth began throwing punches toward the sky, trying to smash his way out of the glop. He kicked, too. His mighty legs nearly broke through, but somehow, the goo managed to stick to the Hulk.

The more he struggled, the more stuck the Hulk seemed to become. He was gasping now, desperately trying to draw oxygen that wasn't there into his gamma-powered lungs. It was getting hard to see, and his world was becoming dark.

He had faced Ultron. The Abomination. Loki.

The most powerful beings in the world (and other worlds, for that matter). And this was how it was going to end. Not with a bang, but with a glop.

The giant thought he heard something then, a noise coming through the ooze that had wrapped itself around his head. It sounded a lot like someone saying, "Get down!"

And that's what the Hulk did. Not that he had a choice, really. He was on the verge of collapse, and collapse he did. With a deafening thud, the behemoth slammed into the desert floor.

With one eye now open, he saw her. A young red-haired woman, dressed in crimson, wearing a black overcoat. She shouldered what looked like a shotgun, pointed right at the Hulk.

No, not at the Hulk.

At the creature?

Hulk heard the shotgun blast, and another sound. A scream? Was he screaming?

No, the ooze was screaming!

The woman fired another blast at the ooze, and suddenly, the Hulk was breathing again.

5

The goo had fallen away from his face, and air rushed into his oxygen-deprived lungs.

"Who . . . ?" asked the Hulk, as the woman continued to blast the strange creature. With every blast, the ooze fell away from the Hulk, until at last, he was free. Something about the shotgun blasts was causing the creature pain and at the same time was also shrinking it. Hulk wasn't sure of much, but he was sure that was no ordinary shotgun.

"Get on your feet and help me contain it!" the woman shouted.

Normally the Hulk wouldn't react kindly to someone yelling at him, but considering that this person had arguably saved his life, he ignored it. The Hulk hefted his massive form, getting to his feet.

The goop tried to slide away from the woman, but the Hulk smashed the ground with his left fist, blocking its path. The vibrations sent the goo scattering.

She fired yet another blast at the goo. And suddenly, it stopped moving.

Was it dead?

"I'm Elsa Bloodstone," said the woman, nodding in the Hulk's direction. "And you have to help me get *that* thing into *this* thing!" She nudged her shotgun toward a metal container – it looked like a giant thermos.

The Hulk scooped the inert goo off the desert floor and put it inside the metal container. When he was done, he handed it to Elsa, who promptly clamped a lid on top, screwing it shut.

"What was that thing?" the Hulk asked.

Elsa stood quietly for a moment as she placed the metal container into a pack she had slung along her back. "I'm not exactly sure," she said. "I'm still in the process of determining its origins. But it's dangerous."

"I think I figured that out already," Hulk said.

Elsa laughed.

• • •

Elsa Bloodstone said her good-byes to the Hulk as the giant coiled his massive legs like springs. Releasing his muscles, the Hulk jumped into the air, disappearing into the sky with a mighty leap.

"Save the world, meet the Hulk," Elsa said.

"My bucket list is looking pretty good."

At that moment, a wall of shimmering energy appeared out of nowhere behind Elsa. She must have expected it, because she walked right into it without a moment's hesitation. She disappeared into the light, and a second later, the energy wall disappeared as well.

Once again, the desert was still.

Except . . .

Except something was moving.

No. Something was oozing.

* * *

Drip.

Drop.

That's how it starts.

With something little. Something so small that our eyes barely notice. Drips and drops, a little here and a little there. Before long, what was small becomes large. And it happens right in front of us. A process so gradual that no one really thinks to say anything until it is far too late.

Which is exactly how IT wanted things to be.

Because, you see, IT could remember. IT remembered what had happened before, when IT was "born" inside a remote castle. IT remembered when IT lived . . . when IT oozed, creeped, and shuffled among the humans. When IT terrified them.

The humans.

How IT hated them. For all it took was one of their number to put an end to IT.

Or so they thought . . .

CHAPTER 1

THE ~~AIR WAS~~ crisp and clean. The ground was still wet from last night's rain. The smell of smoldering leaves wafted through the center of town. Store merchants were just starting to put pumpkins outside their stores.

Fall.

Ben Lee hustled through the town square on his way to school. He was early, but then, he was always early. Since his family had moved from New York City to the tiny town of Highland Park, Ben had come to the quick realization that there wasn't very

much to do here. That's the way it was with small towns. They were quiet and, as his father liked to say, "dull and uneventful." But that was okay with Ben. It gave him some extra time to pursue his passion in life. "Wait up, Ben, or I'll tell Mom!"

Ben sighed. "If you want me to *wait* up, then *hurry* up!" he yelled without looking. He arrived at a covered bus stop on the town square where no bus had stopped in years. Standing opposite the bench in the town square was a large statue of a big man wearing what looked like a parka. Ben supposed it might be the town's founder. Or maybe the town just liked statues of guys wearing parkas.

He sat down on the bench and pulled a black book from his backpack. It was about the size of your average school notebook, and it looked beat-up. Like, really beat-up. One look and you could tell this was a well-loved, treasured item that Ben had toted with him everywhere. On the front cover, in blood red letters, were the words:

MONSTER JOURNAL
PROPERTY OF BEN LEE
DO NOT READ OR YOU WILL
FACE THE WRATH OF
FIN FANG FOOM!

Ben pulled out a pencil and a small pencil sharpener. He twisted the pencil a few times, until it had a good point on it. Then he cracked open his monster journal to a blank page. And he started to draw.

"You're such a dumb big brother some times," said Cindy Lee, huffing a bit as she approached the bus stop. She threw what seemed to be a backpack weighted with rocks or anvils onto the bench, upsetting Ben's book. His pencil tip snapped. Ben huffed.

"And you're such an annoying little sister!" Ben replied. He was only a year and a half older than Cindy. But like most big brothers, he wanted her to remember who was boss. "You broke my pencil!"

"Did not," Cindy said, sitting down.

Ben rolled his eyes, shook his head, and sharpened the pencil again. It wasn't worth having an argument with his sister right now. There was only a little time before they would have to resume their walk to Kurtzberg Middle School. And Ben wanted to use that time wisely. There was a monster that he wanted to capture in his journal.

Cindy sat next to her big brother and watched as he drew what looked like a large dragon with wings. But the dragon appeared to be walking upright, almost like a person.

"Who is that?" Cindy asked. Ben smiled as he sketched.

"It's a monster I read about. It's called Fin Fang Foom."

"Fin Fang Whom?" Cindy asked.

"Foom." Ben laughed. "I read about it last night on *Tales to Astonish*."

Tales to Astonish was talestoastonish.com, a website. But it wasn't just any website. It was Ben's FAVORITE website. It was a message board, devoted to thousands and thousands of threads and pages all

about Ben's best-loved subject: monsters. Nobody knew who ran the website; that part of it was a mystery. But it was an amazing, one-of-a-kind, all-in-one repository of monster knowledge.

"Let me see!" Cindy said, practically ripping the monster journal off Ben's lap. *She can be annoying,* Ben thought, *but she sure does love monsters just as much as I do.* Plus, she was one of the only people who didn't think his monster drawings were completely terrible. Ben wanted to draw just like Kid Kaiju, one of the regulars on the *Tales to Astonish* boards. He seemed to know so much about monsters, almost like they were real! And Kid Kaiju could draw . . . oh, man, could he draw! Much better than Ben could. But that didn't stop Ben from drawing. If anything, it made him try harder.

There they sat, brother and sister, lost in a world of monsters.

That's when IT arrived.

CHAPTER 2

"WELL, WELL, WELL! Look at 'Kid Kaiju' and his big, bad book of monsters!"

Ben's heart sank. He knew that voice. It was worse than the sound of any monster. In fact, he'd rather have been Iron Man facing off against Fin Fang Foom right at that moment than dealing with . . .

"Don Cyphers!" Cindy snapped. She looked up from the monster journal and saw the blocky form of Kurtzberg Middle School's most feared, most obnoxious bully. Don Cyphers was by far the biggest kid at school, with the biggest mouth. *And the smallest brain*, Cindy thought.

"Oooh, what are you gonna do, small fry?" Don

said, smiling. He laughed at his own words, clearly pleased with himself. Don bothered virtually all the kids at Kurtzberg, but he seemed to *really* love picking on Ben. "You gonna call one of your Super Hero friends? Huh? Maybe Spider-Man's gonna come and teach me a lesson!"

Ben had no idea why, but Don really liked to make fun of the fact that Ben had moved from New York City. Everyone knew that New York City was where the Super Heroes lived. Every day, news headlines were full of the exploits of the Avengers, Spider-Man, Ms. Marvel, the Hulk . . . the list went on. For some reason, Don got it in his head that because Ben was from New York City, he thought he was better than the other kids at Kurtzberg Middle School.

Ben did not think this.

And Don did not *think* at all.

So there you have it.

Ben stared at Don, then took the monster journal from his sister. He closed the book and put it in his backpack. Cindy quickly stuck her hand in the backpack, retrieving the monster journal, and put it back on her brother's lap.

"Keep drawing, Ben. Don't let this lamebrain stop you. He wishes he had even *half* of your talent," Cindy said. They might fight like cats and dogs, but he and Cindy always had each other's backs. "And for the record, Cyphers, if Spider-Man *were* here, he'd web your butt to the side of a building."

Don sneered and made a grab for the monster journal. Ben yanked the book away, and Cindy stepped in front of her brother. Now she stood between Ben and the big bully. She was shorter than Ben and much smaller than Don. But Cindy gave off an air that distinctly said, *Mess with me and you will have trouble for the rest of your life.*

"Don't you have better things to do than get beat up by me?" Cindy said. She balled her hands into fists and gave Don a fierce look. Ben knew that look. On more than one occasion, he'd found out the hard way what came after that look. . . .

Suddenly, there was the sound of screeching tires. And then a deep voice: "You're not supposed to be here right now. You're really in for it!"

CHAPTER 3

A BLACK-AND-WHITE POLICE

car had pulled up on the street right in front of the kids. Looking at them from the driver's side of the car was Sheriff Cyphers – Don's dad. And he didn't look happy.

"Dad!" Don shouted, pulling himself away from Ben and Cindy. "I was just, uh, saying hi to my friends before I – "

Sheriff Cyphers gave Don a look that said, *I'm not buying what you're selling*. He opened the door of the police car and got out. He stood, looking over the top of the car at Don, Ben, and Cindy.

"Well, it's almost time for school, kid.

Why don't you and your 'friends' keep walking? Otherwise you're going to be late, and then I'll have to throw the lot of you Super Villains in jail," Sheriff Cyphers said sternly.

The kids looked at the police officer. Was he serious?

Then, Sheriff Cyphers broke out in a broad grin, and started to laugh. "I'm only kidding! You'd have to do a lot more than that to end up in *my* jail," he said. "But seriously, you should all get to school before I call your parents . . . or tell your mom." Sheriff Cyphers directed the last part at Don, and arched an eyebrow at his son.

Don huffed and hurried off, but turned around and looked at Ben. He mouthed the words *This isn't over!* Cindy shook a fist at the bully.

Ben sighed. It was like this every day. It figured that the sheriff's son would be the biggest bully in town. And as far as Ben was concerned, Don Cyphers *was* a Super Villain. Worse than the Green Goblin, Red Skull, and Loki rolled into one. Why couldn't Sheriff Cyphers put Don in jail? Just to, you know, teach him a lesson?

"Everything okay, you two?" asked the sheriff. "Was my son bugging you again?"

"It's fine," said Cindy. "I can handle him."

The Sheriff chuckled loudly. "I have no doubt," he said, smiling. "Well, you let me know. Get to school now. Give your mom my best." Then Sheriff Cyphers hopped back into his police car and drove away. Don Cyphers may have been a bully, but his dad was a good guy. He certainly had his hands full with Don.

"He's right, we should get going," Ben said as he picked up the monster journal and put it safely in his backpack. "And thanks, Cindy."

Cindy grinned as the pair left the bus stop and headed down the sidewalk toward school.

"Anytime, big brother. Now tell me more about Fin Fang Foom. . . ."

"Okay, so check it! I was reading about him last night on *Tales to Astonish*! He fought off the Chinese army, and nobody thought he could be stopped! Except a guy figured out how to make him go to sleep!" Ben babbled excitedly.

"Wow, sleep! Really? That sounds super exciting!" Cindy said with mock amazement in her voice. "Tell me again how the day was saved by napping!"

"But that's how it happened! I'm sorry, I don't make this stuff up," Ben said. "Not every giant monster story has chases and battles and excitement, ya know."

The kids walked along the town square and headed toward the school. Neither bothered to look down at their feet. And why would they? If they had, all they would have noticed was concrete, dirt, bubble gum, and goo.

Goo, bubbling up through the cracks in the pavement.

Goo that pulsed.

Like it was . . . alive?

CHAPTER 4

SOMETHING WAS BUBBLING and oozing. It had no eyes, but it stared right up at Ben. It seemed to be creeping closer and closer to him! He turned his head, panicked, trying to avoid the inevitable.

"It's going to get me!" Ben shrieked. "It's going to . . . eat me!"

"Oh, come on, Ben, it's not that bad!" said his mother. She pointed at the plate in front of him. The plate had some kind of orange blob on it that Mrs. Lee claimed was their dinner.

Ben didn't believe it.

"You're always trying new recipes!" Ben moped, pushing the orange glob around on his plate with

a fork. "Why can't we just have *galbi jjim*? This feels more like punishment than dinner."

Galbi jjim was Ben's favorite – braised beef short ribs. Ben loved the Korean dishes his mom made. She was an awesome cook. He could happily eat his mom's galbi jjim and her *jjajangmyun* – black bean sauce and noodles – forever.

But whatever was on the plate in front of him now was pure culinary evil.

"New is good!" Mrs. Lee answered. "You should try new things. You never know, you may like them." Mrs. Lee turned toward Cindy, who was dutifully eating everything on her plate, smiling. "See? Your sister likes it."

Cindy smiled an insincere smile at Ben. He groaned.

"She doesn't really like it, Mom. She's just pretending she does so I get in trouble."

"Well, you won't *get* in trouble if you eat your dinner," Mrs. Lee said.

"What is 'dinner,' exactly?" Ben asked.

His mom tilted her head to one side, looking at

23

her plate. "It's tuna casserole."

"And what's this on top of it?" Ben said, pointing at the bumpy orange surface of his "food."

"It's cornflakes. You know, the cereal."

Ben groaned. He wasn't sure why his mom insisted on making gross things like tuna casserole with cornflakes when there was a fridge full of perfectly good kimchi to be eaten.

He stared at his plate as his mom finished her meal. Cindy finished hers as well, leaving Ben alone at the table to confront the orange blob on his plate.

"What would Kid Kaiju do?" Ben wondered aloud. He put down his fork and tried picking up the orange blob with his spoon instead. That seemed to work better.

"He'd probably draw a picture of it in his monster journal," Cindy chimed in. This broke up Ben, who couldn't stop laughing. Maybe Kid Kaiju would, maybe he wouldn't. But Ben knew what *he* was going to do.

Deciding that the sooner he ate, the sooner the nightmare of the orange blob dinner would be a distant memory, Ben held his nose. Spoonful after spoonful, he shoveled the orange blob into his mouth. It wasn't as bad as Ben thought it would be.

It was worse.

At last he finished. Plates went into the sink, and they headed upstairs.

It was time for bed, but Ben wasn't ready for sleep, as usual. It was lights-out time (9:00 p.m. sharp, as his mom always said), and Ben followed the rule. But that didn't mean he couldn't switch on his tiny reading lamp. He sat at his drawing desk, the one his mom had given him for his last birthday. The monster journal was open, and Ben was busy writing. He had already drawn a picture of an enormous orange blob, attacking the town square.

"Is that mom's din – ?"

"Ahhhhh!" Ben screamed. He whirled around, only to find his sister inches away from his face. "At least make some noise when you sneak into my room! You scared the snot out of me!"

"I did? Good!" Ben's sister replied. "Speaking of snot, is that mom's dinner?" She pointed at the monster journal.

Ben loosened up and turned the journal so Cindy could see it. "Yeah, I figured it deserved monster status. Want to see what else I've been working on?"

Cindy gave her brother a look that said *As if you had to ask*, and they were off and running. Pages flipped and jaws dropped as Cindy gaped and howled and pointed at all the different monsters that Ben had been adding to his journal.

"Pretty scary, right?" said Ben. As Cindy flipped through the journal bathed in the light of the reading lamp, Ben tried to make some spooky sounds.

"MoooooAAAAAhhhhhhAaaaHhaaaaa!"

"You sound like a sleepy chimp," Cindy said.

"Really?" Ben frowned. "Not even a *little* scary?" Cindy shook her head.

"What are you still doing up?! It's nine thirty!" Mrs. Lee shouted from downstairs. "Lights out! Even your reading light, Ben! And go to your own room, Cindy!"

Ben and Cindy sighed and then, in unison, yelled, "Okay, Mom!" Cindy padded out of Ben's room and went across the hall to her own bedroom.

He shut off the reading light and headed toward his bed. He pulled the covers up over his head and pulled out a small, pocket-size flashlight he kept hidden under his pillow. And then he pulled something else out from under his pillow – a thick hardcover book with a beat-up dust jacket. The book was called *The Bloodstone Chronicles: The Bloodstone Family and the Search for Monsters*. It was one of his most prized possessions. It had made the move from New York City to Highland Park in the same backpack as his monster journal.

Ben was just about to turn on his pocket flashlight and reread one of his favorite books about monster hunting, when the light in his room came back on.

Ben let out a loud, exaggerated sigh. All he wanted to do was be left alone to read his book in secret, and Cindy was going to ruin it by getting Mom mad.

"Cindy, Mom said we have to – "

As Ben turned around, he saw the reading light was, in fact, off. So was his bedroom light. The light hadn't come back on. Cindy wasn't there. It was coming from somewhere else.

Cindy ran back into Ben's room, excitedly. "Look!" she said. "Do you see the light coming from outside?" She stood by Ben's bedroom window, looking out toward the center of town. An eerie glow emanated from it and pulsed a few times, before disappearing entirely.

"What *was* that?" Cindy asked, excited.

"I . . . don't know," Ben gasped. "But I think I know who would."

CHAPTER 5

IT WAS ~~DARK~~, and he sat at his desk. There was a lone lamp providing just enough light to sketch by. The desk was littered with pieces of paper. And on each, there was a pencil drawing.

Of a monster.

Some of them were monsters he had read about in books, like Zzutak and Spoor. Some he had seen on the news – like the time the mighty Thor had fought Fin Fang Foom. He wasn't sure what some of the other ones were called – as far as he knew, some of the monsters he drew were just products of his imagination, curious creatures brought forth from the back of his mind. Kei had two passions: art and monsters. Right now, in this moment, he was in the zone.

"Kei!" came a voice from downstairs. "Are you still up? It's a school night, shouldn't you be in bed?"

Mom.

Kei sighed. He knew his mom was right, but he just *had* to get this monster down on paper.

"Just a few more minutes, Mom!" Kei yelled down. "I'm almost done!"

He turned his attention back to his drawing. The pencil clutched in his right hand moved slowly, deliberately across the page. Kei had been drawing for years and had learned to take his time. He wanted to make sure that what he was seeing in his mind was captured perfectly on the page.

Kei took a break from his drawing to look over at a nearby computer screen. He was looking at a website, one that he loved to follow – *Tales to Astonish*. There were countless threads about unsolved mysteries, myths, and cryptids. Most of the time, he was just regular ol' Kei. But when logged on to *Tales to Astonish*, he was something else – Kid Kaiju, expert on all things supernatural!

Especially monsters.

"I'm not kidding, Kei! Lights out!"

"Okay, Mom!" Kei shouted. He was just about done with his drawing anyway. He erased a couple of lines, then took the piece of paper in hand. He stuck a piece of transparent tape on each corner, then put it on his bedroom wall.

Taking a step back before turning out the light, Kei admired his handiwork: a picture of a large blob, sort of shaped like a giant person, leaving a trail of . . .

Glop.

CHAPTER 6

"WAIT UP, CINDY, or I'll tell Mom!" Ben shouted at his sister, who was running ahead of him – WAY ahead of him. Neither could wait to walk toward the center of town on the way to school. They both were curious to see where that eerie glow may have been coming from. They had breakfast early, made their lunches, said good-bye to their mom, and headed out the door.

By the time they had reached the town square, Ben had caught up to his sister. It was early, around 7:00 a.m., and they were surprised to see some other kids from school there. Ben wondered if maybe they had witnessed the same strange light that he and

Cindy had seen last night. They were standing near the bus stop, and looking at something in the middle of the square directly opposite.

It was the statue – the same statue that the kids saw every day on their way to school. Only something was different. If Ben didn't know any better, he'd swear that – overnight – the statue had moved!

No, not like it had moved; it was still in the same spot. More like it had changed positions. The arms that were once raised up were now lower, pointing toward the ground. Was this some kind of prank? Ben looked around for a hidden camera, but didn't see one.

The statue was unremarkable except for its size and its weird, hunched-over pose.

"Is that a different statue?" Cindy asked, examining the strange figure.

"I don't think so," Ben said. "I mean, the face looks the same, and it's the same dopey parka."

"But look at its arms," Cindy replied. "They look . . . different!"

Ben whipped out his phone and snapped a picture.

33

"I'll post this to *Tales to Astonish*," he said, uploading the photo to the website. "Maybe somebody there will know a thing or two about statues that suddenly move overnight."

"You can add it to your journal, too," Cindy said. "A moving statue is freaky enough to belong next to the rest of your monsters!"

The other kids turned their attention from the statue and saw Ben typing away on his phone, while Cindy reached into his backpack. She pulled out the monster journal, with its blood red letters on the cover, and handed it to Ben. He put the phone away, pulled a pencil out his jacket pocket, and started to sketch the statue as the other kids watched.

"Hey, you're pretty good," said a kid with a high-pitched, nasal voice.

At last – someone who appreciates my talent, Ben thought.

"What's it supposed to be?" the same kid added.

So much for art appreciation, Ben thought, shaking his head.

"Maybe it's Mr. Pierce," said a kid with a mouth

stuffed full of breakfast bar. He snort-laughed and spat little crumbs out of his mouth.

This broke the kids up. Even Ben had to laugh a little. Mr. Pierce was the art teacher at Kurtzberg Middle School. He was also the OLDEST teacher at Kurtzberg Middle School. The students were pretty sure that he must have started teaching when the school first opened. In 1901. Sure, he was weird and kind of mean and a little freaky and did this thing with his false teeth that grossed everybody out, but none of that bothered Ben. The guy was a pretty talented artist in his own right. If you could look past all the goofy stuff, you could actually learn something from him.

Before long, Ben had drawn the statue in his journal. The kids were transfixed until one of them realized they had about five minutes to get to school before the first bell. Everyone ran off, including Ben and Cindy, leaving the statue by itself.

Alone.

Except for the glop that bubbled up from the pavement beneath it . . .

CHAPTER 7

"WHAT DO YOU think happened?"

"Did someone switch the statue in the middle of the night?"

"Who put it there?"

"The Hulk?"

"Seriously? You think the Hulk doesn't have better things to do than replace statues in our dinky town?"

"Well, the statue looks pretty heavy. Who else could have lifted it?"

"Maybe, like, Red Hulk?"

"If the Hulk wasn't gonna show up in our town, there's no way Red Hulk would!"

The art room at Kurtzberg Middle School was abuzz with voices as Ben and his classmates talked about the mysterious moving statue in the town square. No one paid attention to their art projects.

"Ben's from New York; he's the Super Hero expert," said one of the kids. "What do you think happened, Ben?"

Ben sighed. "I don't know how this rumor got started that I'm some kind of Super Hero expert! Just because I'm from New York doesn't mean I know everything there is to know about Super Heroes!" Then he thought for a minute. "Yeah, there's no way Hulk did this. He's on an Avengers mission, saw it on the news."

"Put a cork in it!" said Mr. Pierce, the art teacher, and the class fell silent. "Back to your still life projects!" he barked, pointing to a lone bowl full of plastic oranges sitting in front of the classroom. "I don't care what you saw, where you saw it, or if you were riding a pony while dressed in a bunny suit while seeing it. I only want to see fruit, bowls, and more fruit!"

"But there's only oranges," said one student.

"So?" Mr. Pierce said. "Use your imagination! That bowl's full of apples and mangoes and that fruit, you know, the one that's really stinky!"

The class stared at Mr. Pierce.

"Uh, which stinky fruit?" someone asked.

"The one that stinks!"

"Durian fruit?" someone said.

"Sure! That one! Now draw!"

Ben put his head down and started to sketch. But instead of the plastic oranges, he began to sketch the statue on the blank piece of paper in front of him. *Man, that really is weird*, he thought. The arms were longer than he remembered, now that he thought about it. And the way they were reaching toward the ground. Reaching for what?

"And what do you think you are you drawing, Ben?" Mr. Pierce asked, peering over the boy's shoulder. "It looks an awful lot like not a bowl of fruit."

"Uh, sorry, Mr. Pierce," Ben said. "It's the statue. The one from town that everybody's talking about."

Mr. Pierce lowered his glasses and squinted at

Ben's still life. But instead of getting angry, like he always did, Mr. Pierce muttered something under his breath. "Not again." Then suddenly Mr. Pierce pulled the false teeth from his mouth and gave them a wipe with his handkerchief. He popped the teeth back in his mouth.

It was always disturbing whenever Mr. Pierce took out his teeth. No one was sure why he did that, exactly, and it was gross.

"What do you mean, 'Not again'?" Ben asked.

Mr. Pierce stood for a moment, silent, staring right at Ben. He blinked.

"What?" he said, as if he hadn't heard or didn't understand what Ben was talking about.

"You said 'Not again' when you saw the picture of the statue," Ben continued. "What did you mean?"

"Are you talking back to me?" Mr. Pierce said, flustered. "Never mind. Forget about it. Just draw. Draw that fruit! I wanna see fruit!" The art teacher stormed off, sat down at his desk, and popped his teeth out again, holding them in his right hand.

Gross.

But that wasn't what made Ben feel uneasy at that moment. He wondered what Mr. Pierce had meant by *Not again*. And why the old art teacher had dodged Ben's question.

Did Mr. Pierce know the secret of the strange moving statue?

CHAPTER 8

RECESS. While the other kids played kickball and just generally hung out, Ben sat on the stoop with his monster journal on his lap and a pencil in his right hand. He stared at the picture he had drawn of the statue. It was still the town founder or parka guy or whoever it was, but there was something almost inhuman about it. The way the arms stretched out. They were just . . . wrong. Ben couldn't seem to get it out of his mind.

What he *really* wanted to do was check the *Tales to Astonish* website to see if anyone had responded to his photo yet. But the school had a strict "no cell phones during school hours" policy. The last kid who tried to use his phone during recess had it taken away from him.

"Hey, nerd."

Ben looked up to see the last kid who tried to use his phone during recess.

Don Cyphers stood over Ben, leering. He was breathing through his mouth, which was usual for Don. His lips were curled in a cruel smile as he poked at Ben's monster journal.

"Whatcha drawing in your monster book? Something dumb?" Don chortled. That was a particularly bright, insightful insult coming from him.

"Well, I'm not drawing you, if that's what you're asking," Ben said. He stood up from the stoop, then started to walk away. *Better to find another place to sit down,* Ben thought. Maybe the school should set up a "Don-Free Zone."

Don didn't even listen, but he followed Ben and kept right on talking. "I bet it's that dumb statue from the town square." *Dumb* was Don's favorite word. "I'll bet that dumb ol' Mr. Pierce switched it."

The old art teacher lived on the outskirts of town, in a ramshackle house on top of Mount Minor. Mount Minor wasn't really much of a mountain or a mount. It was barely a hill. Still, by town standards, it was big.

"Why do you think Mr. Pierce put it there?" Ben asked. Did Don know something about the art teacher that he didn't? It sure didn't seem likely, but hey, you never know.

"Because he likes dumb art and doing dumb things," Don said.

Ben sighed. "You know everything," he said.

"I know, right? That's what my dad tells me."

The recess bell rang as Don made a grab for the monster journal with a meaty hand. Ben yanked it away. Don sniffed and wandered inside with the other kids.

It's crazy, but could Don be right? Ben thought. *Could Mr. Pierce be the one behind the statue?*

CHAPTER 9

IT SEEMED LIKE school lasted about thirty hours that day instead of the usual six and a half. In fact, it felt like Mrs. Rubin's science class had taken about twenty-five of those hours. Ben liked Mrs. Rubin well enough, and he liked science. But he didn't like having Don Cyphers in his class. All he did was bug Ben, get in trouble, and ask when they were going to make baking soda volcanoes.

Finally, Ben and his sister were walking home, toward the town square.

"Did anyone respond yet?" Cindy asked excitedly. Ben knew she was talking about his post on *Tales to Astonish*. Ben shook his head.

The first thing he had done when they left

school was to check *Tales to Astonish* on his phone. "Not yet. I was hoping someone would have posted *something* by now. . . ." His voice trailed off.

"'Someone,' like Kid Kaiju?"

Ben grinned. "Yeah, that would be something. But come on, there's no way he's going to see this. He's got to be super busy. Besides, he's, like, a big shot in the monster world. He's never going to notice me."

"Are you kidding? You're Ben Lee, New York's Super Hero expert and Highland Park's resident monster master!"

Ben laughed.

When they arrived at the town square, they saw the townspeople going about their business as usual. Sheriff Cyphers was there, helping to direct what little traffic the town had. And there was the statue, right where Ben and Cindy had left it.

Except it looked different, somehow.

Like the statue had changed positions. Again.

Its "hands" were now touching the ground.

But how? If someone had actually replaced the

45

statue at night, how did they pull off the same thing in broad daylight? It didn't make any sense!

"Looks a little different this afternoon, doesn't it?" said Sheriff Cyphers, pushing back his hat. He looked at the statue and shook his head. "I don't know much about art, but I know what I like. I don't like it."

"It's kinda weird," Ben said. It was more than *kind of* weird. It was *super* weird. A statue that stood in one position one minute, then in another the next? What was going on here?

And as they were entranced by the weirdness of the statue that had seemingly moved, neither Ben nor Cindy nor anyone else noticed the little puddle of ooze that had slowly appeared near the statue.

The puddle that glowed.

CHAPTER 10

HE HAD MADE IT home in record time. Not that he didn't like school – he loved it. But what Kei *really* wanted was to get back to his room, his drawings, and his world of monsters. The creature he was drawing last night, the one that left all the glop behind it . . . something about the drawing had caught his interest. He couldn't put his finger on it, but he felt there was something familiar about it.

Had he read about this monster somewhere before?

His first stop was his bookshelf. He had all kinds of volumes on the subject of monsters. These were the kind of books he had loved since he could remember.

Whenever he went to the library, he would check out the same monster books over and over and over. It drove Kei's mom crazy, but at least he was reading.

Kei pulled a weather-beaten book off the shelf with the title *The Bloodstone Chronicles: The Bloodstone Family and the Search for Monsters*. This was one of Kei's go-to books whenever he needed some quick info on a monster. He flipped the pages and did a picture walk through the book but didn't find anything.

The gears in Kei's mind started to whirl and click, and he hopped over to his computer and logged in to the *Tales to Astonish* website. If it wasn't in his books, maybe he could find the answer here. He bypassed the message-board tab and went straight to another one, marked MONSTER LORE. That was the history part of the website – a virtual encyclopedia of all different kinds of monsters from across the globe and history. It was Kei's favorite part of *Tales to Astonish*, where he could learn all about strange, new creatures.

Monster Lore had its own search function, so Kei typed in one word:

48

GLOP

He pressed Return on the keyboard and waited. A few seconds later, a screen came up showing 198 different hits for *glop*. Kei scrolled through them, looking for anything, any detail that might catch his eye. Most of the entries were about big, apelike monsters with tails that drooled a lot and left "glop" – in this case, ape drool – behind.

"I did not come here to read about ape drool," Kei said out loud as he continued to scroll through the search results. It seemed like the search was going nowhere, until he saw an entry near the end. It wasn't the word *glop* that grabbed him, though.

It was a name.

Elsa Bloodstone.

Kei's eyes nearly bulged out of his skull when he saw the name. He knew about Elsa Bloodstone! She came from a family of monster hunters. They were the subject of the book he had just been looking at – *The Bloodstone Chronicles: The Bloodstone Family and the Search for Monsters*. Elsa's father, Ulysses Bloodstone, had been a monster hunter for years – some even believed that he was hundreds of years old! There was a rumor that he had once called himself Ahab and went off in search of a giant whalelike creature, and that was the basis for the book *Moby Dick*. Kei wasn't sure whether or not he believed that one, but he did know that the Bloodstones were the real deal. If Elsa Bloodstone's name was attached to a search about this "glop," Kei had to find out more.

He clicked on the search link, and the page opened before him.

Kei was shocked to see nearly the same creature he had sketched the previous night staring back at him from the computer screen. The entry had been written by an anonymous *Tales to Astonish* user, but they quoted extensively from notes written by Elsa Bloodstone. Kei's pulse raced. This was incredible!

Kid Kaiju couldn't believe it – it was like he was working with Elsa Bloodstone!

CHAPTER 11

BEN AND HIS SISTER were walking home down the tree-lined street when they noticed it. Actually, it was Cindy who noticed it first. Her shoes were making a "thwuck-thwuck" sound whenever they hit the pavement. It was an annoying sound, and it was slowly driving her nuts.

"What's on my shoes? What did we walk through?" Cindy asked, causing Ben to snap out of his monster dreams.

"What are you talking about?" Ben replied. He looked down at Cindy's feet, and that's when he saw it. An orange-ish glop that seemed stuck on the soles of her shoes. Ben stared at his own shoes and saw that they had the same glop on them. *It looks like we have been hiking through the swamp with the Man-Thing*, Ben thought.

They walked a few more steps, and again there was the "thwuck-thwuck" sound.

"Get that gunk off your shoes," Cindy said. "I can't stand that sound. Gross!"

Both kids scraped the soles of their shoes against the curb, and the glop seemed to come off. They looked behind them and saw they had left a trail of gloppy footprints all down the sidewalk.

"You know this is getting *way* too weird, right?" Cindy said.

"Oh, yeah," Ben said. He snapped a few pictures of the gloppy footprints with his cell phone. "I think we should upload these to *Tales to Astonish*, too. Man, I wish we could actually talk to Kid Kaiju. He might know what this is all about."

Cindy nodded. "I wish it was a giant monster, but that would be too cool for this town," she said. "Let's get home. We need to be living, breathing, and eating *Tales to Astonish*!"

"What about our homework?" Ben asked. "We better do it first, or Mom is gonna kill us."

Cindy glared at him. "Seriously?" she said.

"I know, it sounded dumb as soon as it came out of my mouth. Homework, shmomework. *Tales to Astonish* it is!"

The kids and their now glop-free shoes headed for home.

If only they had waited just a few seconds longer, they would have seen something far stranger than just gloppy footprints.

They would have seen the glop they had scraped off on the curb peel itself away from the cement.

And then it rolled.

It rolled toward the first set of gloppy footprints. The glop oozed into the footprint until it became a part of it. Then *that* glop peeled itself off the pavement and rolled to the next footprint. It became a slightly bigger ball of glop, then rolled to the next footprint. Which oozed a few inches to the next gloppy footprint.

And so on . . . and so on . . .

CHAPTER 17

"**CLOSE THE DOOR** so Mom doesn't see the light!" Ben shout-whispered. "How is it possible that *you* never get in trouble when you're the one who's always doing stuff?"

Cindy rolled her eyes, shook her head, and quietly closed Ben's bedroom door. "Happy now?" she said. Ben grumbled and turned back to the computer. The *Tales to Astonish* home page stared back at him as Ben clicked through the various threads, searching. His stomach rumbled. They had purple blobs for dinner, which his mom claimed was something called "eggplant surprise." He feigned a stomachache to get out of eating it. Now he was hungry and silently wishing for a plate of kimchi *jeon* – kimchi pancakes.

"What are you looking for?" Cindy said. Ben glared at her, and she immediately made an *Oops, sorry!* face. Then she continued, her voice hushed this time. "I keep forgetting to whisper."

"Well, *don't* forget! If we wake up Mom, she's gonna have a fit." Ben continued scanning the website. "Anyway, I'm searching for any info on the statue. Maybe someone's responded to the photo I uploaded."

"See if it says anything about gloppy footprints!" Cindy whispered, excitedly.

"You can't just search for 'gloppy footprints,'" Ben said. "That's not how the search engine works!"

"I bet that's *exactly* how it works," Cindy said, pushing her older brother away from the keyboard. Before he could do anything, Cindy had typed "gloppy footprints" into the *Tales to Astonish* search window.

"Hey!" Ben interjected. "I was typing! Besides, you're not gonna get any . . ."

Cindy pointed at the computer screen, a broad

grin on her face. The first hit she got revealed a thread called:

GLOPPY FOOTPRINTS???

". . . results."

Ben pushed his sister away from the computer, then clicked on the link, which took him to a new thread. Beneath the words "Gloppy Footprints???" there was a thumbnail picture of something monstrous. It was kind of shaped like a huge person, but it was amorphous, like a blob. It was shambling, oozing along, leaving a trail of gloppy footprints behind it.

"Whoa!" both kids shouted in unison. Their eyes went wide, and each clamped a hand over the other's mouth. They hoped their outburst wouldn't wake up their mom!

"Ben, gloppy footprints! That looks like the glop that was on the bottom of our shoes!" Cindy said.

Ben nodded. "This is so freaky," he agreed. He clicked on the thumbnail image, which took him to a page in *Tales to Astonish*'s Monster Lore section. He scanned the page quickly, but before he could start reading the article, an eerie glow filled the room.

"The light!" Ben said, as he and his sister moved to the window. "There it is again." Looking toward the town square, they saw the same strange light they had witnessed the other night. The glow pulsed just as it had before, like a heart beating.

"What do you think it is?" Cindy asked.

"I don't know," Ben replied. He jumped away from the window, opened his dresser drawer, and pulled out a flashlight. He pressed the button and waved his hand in front of it to make sure it still worked.

"Suit up!" he said. "Let's go find out!"

CHAPTER 13

IT WAS ~~PAST~~ MIDNIGHT when Ben and Cindy sneaked out of their house. Their mom was long asleep, and they were careful not to step on any creaky stairs or bang any doors on the way out. There was a chill in the air, and each wore sweatpants, a hooded sweatshirt, and sneakers. The beam from Ben's flashlight illuminated the street as they walked into town. In the distance, they could see the glow coming from the town square.

"I still can't believe this town doesn't have streetlights everywhere," Cindy said, shaking her head.

"Why would they?" Ben answered. "Nobody in this town goes out after ten o'clock."

"I also can't believe you said 'Suit up.' Like we're the Avengers or something."

Ben laughed. "I should have shouted 'Ben and Cindy, assemble!' Would that have been better?"

Cindy looked at her brother. "Worse. You would have woken up Mom *and* you would have sounded like a bigger nerd than you already are."

The kids followed the same path they had taken on their walk home from school. That's when Cindy noticed it.

"The footprints," she said quietly. She pointed to the sidewalk beneath them.

"What?"

"The footprints," she said, more insistent. "*Our* footprints. The gloppy ones, from this afternoon."

"What about 'em?" Ben said, looking ahead toward the town square, now in view. The eerie glow continued to pulsate from the location.

"They're not here anymore," she said. "They're *gone.*"

"So what?" Ben said. "The street cleaner probably took care of them." Then he thought about that for a minute. "Except this rinky-dink town probably doesn't *have* a street cleaner. Okay, that's another weird thing to put on the list."

They walked down the street and saw a police car parked outside of a gray house with a dark blue roof. That was Sheriff Cyphers's home. Ben looked up at the house and its darkened windows. "It's hard to believe that right now, even as we speak, Don Cyphers is inside that house, sleeping like an angel," he said.

Cindy laughed. "More like a devil," she added. "Seriously, why do you let that clown get to you? He's just jealous of you."

Ben thought about it for a second as they walked past the house. "I don't know," he started. "Maybe because he could crush my head like a nut?"

"He could not," Cindy jumped in. "If he so much as looked at you funny, I'd deck him."

"Yeah, you probably would," Ben said. "But remember – with great power, there must also come great responsibility!"

"Oooh, that's a good one. I'll have to remember

that," Cindy said.

Soon enough, Ben and Cindy were in the center of town. It was desolate, quiet – and there wasn't another soul around. They finally saw the source of the glow.

The statue.

"Wait, does that statue look different to you?" said Cindy.

Ben raised his eyebrows and nodded vigorously.

It was true. Somehow, the statue had changed positions again. Now it looked like both of its "arms" were raised up, as if it were about to grab something.

"Look!" Ben shouted. "It's not the statue that's glowing – it's what's beneath the statue!"

That's when both kids saw the glop – glowing, bright orange – begin to ooze out from the pavement beneath the statue. It squeezed out of the cracks, until a puddle of it had formed on the ground. Then, more than a puddle. It pooled up all around the statue and began to flow onto it. The goo seemed to have a life all its own as it swooped and swirled in the air. The glop crept up the statue's

"legs" as Ben and Cindy watched.

"This is absolutely freaky," Cindy said. "You're getting pictures of this, right?"

Cindy didn't need to ask. Ben stood right next to her, phone in hand, snapping away.

"I am getting pictures of this," Ben said. "And I am wondering why we are not running. Shouldn't we be running?"

The glop continued to flow all around the statue, until it had covered it completely. Somehow, more glop oozed out from the cracks in the pavement below, and rose up the statue. It looked bigger now, almost like it was growing.

And then it moved.

CHAPTER 14

"WE HAVE A REAL live monster in our town!" Cindy shouted, punching her big brother on his left arm.

"Ow!" Ben said, rubbing the spot on his arm. "Did you have to punch me?"

"Yes! I did! Because it is *that* exciting!" Cindy said.

Ben took more pictures with his phone. "*Exciting* isn't even the word for it. It's amazing, unbelievable . . . astonishing!"

The massive, glop-covered statue continued to move, its arms lowering to its side. Then the thing's head turned.

Toward Ben.

It seemed to stare right at him. Its "face" was a swirl of slime that seemed to shift every few seconds. The slime dripped from its "face" and onto the ground. Then the Glop bubbled and rolled along the ground, back onto the thing's body.

Ben was transfixed by the sight. The Glop seemed to pulse with a life all its own. It had somehow become one with the creepy statue. Like it had absorbed it – Ben couldn't even see the statue inside the Glop anymore.

It was alive!

"Look out!" Cindy cried as she pushed her brother out of the way of a massive, glop-covered fist! The fist slammed right into the spot where they had been standing. The Glop picked up its fist from the ground, then took steps – actual steps! – toward Ben and Cindy.

"What the what?!" Ben yelled. "That thing is coming right for us!"

The massive mound of shambling glop staggered toward Ben and Cindy. It lurched, somehow walking and oozing at the same time. As it moved across the ground, it left a trail of slimy footprints behind it.

Ben and Cindy looked at each other as they both screamed, "RUN!"

CHAPTER 15

IT'S ~~AMAZING~~ just how fast a pair of feet can carry you when you're afraid. That's what was racing through Ben's mind as he and his sister made tracks away from the town square. He stole a brief glance over his shoulder, and he saw the shambling mound behind him. The Glop was moving toward them.

It wasn't a dream.

It wasn't even a nightmare, although Ben wished it were.

No, it was real. And it was coming after him and Cindy!

"Hhhhhhuuuuuuu" came a low, rumbling sound from the town square.

"Was that – ?" Cindy began.

"I think it was – " Ben added, before he was interrupted by further sounds.

"Hhhhhhhuuuuumannnsssss!"

Ben and Cindy stopped in their tracks.

"Did that thing just talk?!" Cindy asked.

Ben nodded. Both he and his sister looked behind them. Lurching from the town square, slowly, coming toward them, was the massive, oozing form. It seemed to have a face, sort of, and a mouth, kind of. As its "mouth" opened, another sound came out: "Yyyoouuu aaarrrrrrrrre dooooooooomed!"

"Did that thing just say we're doomed?!" Cindy asked again.

Ben nodded, his head barely moving.

They sprinted away.

It's amazing just how fast a pair of feet can carry you when you're afraid.

o o o

"How does that thing move so fast?" Ben questioned. He was panting as he ran, his sister right next to him. Somehow, the giant blob of whatever-it-was had managed to keep pace with the kids. It hadn't caught up to them yet, but it was right behind them. Ben swung his arms as he sprinted, like he was trying to grab the air in front of him and pull himself forward.

"Can we call it something else instead of a 'thing'?" Cindy said, shouting over the sound of their sneakers hitting the pavement.

They kept on running. Ahead of them, they saw a stand of trees. The edge of a forest right outside of town. Maybe they could lose the thing in there? It was worth a try.

"Yyyyoooour misssserabbble tooooowwwwwnnnn willll falllll befffoooooore usssss" came a voice from behind them. The creature. The sounds that came from its "mouth" were truly horrifying – it didn't sound like a person. It was like a creaky door being opened slowly, mixed with the bubbling sounds of a pot of boiling water. A gross parody of a person.

"Yoooooooouuuuurrr toooowwwwwnnnn . . . annnnnnnddddd thennnnnnnn . . . thhhhheeeeee woooooooorrrrrlllldddddd!"

Well, sure, Ben thought. *You have to take over the town before you take over the world, that only makes sense.*

The monster continued moving, dragging itself along the ground, leaving a trail of slimy footprints in its wake. Ben and Cindy kept on running. Now they were breathing so hard, their sides hurt. But they had to stay ahead of it. They had to make it to the trees. To safety.

As if anywhere would be safe.

"Rrrrruuunnnnnn wwwwhillleee yoooouuuuu caaaaaannnnn," the thing spat. "Wwweeee willlllll geeeeet yooouuuuu beffffooooooreeee yooooouuuu caaann waaaaarrrnnnnn annnyyyyonnne. . . ."

CHAPTER 16

"THE GLOP," Kei said to himself as he stared at the computer screen. He had spent the last hour reading the *Tales to Astonish* entry on the monster and Elsa Bloodstone's notes about it. There wasn't much to go on, but at least Kei had a name – and a little bit of background now.

So he was surprised – but not very – when he saw a thread on the *Tales to Astonish* message board started by a user named benthemonsterkid:

benthemonsterkid:
WHAT IS THIS? NEED HELP!

benthemonsterkid:
Our town statue (Parka Guy) seemed to move overnight! Anyone know anything about weird moving statues?

Then, in the same thread, there was another post from benthemonsterkid:

benthemonsterkid:
And now this gooey glop. Anyone ever seen anything like this before?

The user had uploaded a couple of blurry photographs, and Kei quickly downloaded them to his desktop. Then he went back to the anonymous article all about the Glop. In addition to the sketch of the gloppy monster, there was a mention of a statue. A statue of an ordinary person. As he kept reading, he learned that the statue seemed to move on its own.

Everything that benthemonsterkid was describing fit the article's description of the Glop.

"Ben the monster kid," Kei said out loud, as he started to type. "You are in trouble, my friend. And you're gonna need help, Kid Kaiju–style."

KidKaiju:
That thing is called the Glop. You need to get away from it as fast as you can. . . .

CHAPTER 17

THE FOREST AT NIGHT. Clouds overhead. The ground, slick with moisture. Fog rolling in. Strange sounds all around. Like something out of a horror movie.

Only it wasn't a horror movie.

It was real.

And Ben and Cindy Lee were stuck smack-dab in the middle of it.

Ben and Cindy were slumped against the back of an enormous oak tree in the forest. They were sweaty, panting, trying to catch their breath. How long had they been running? Ben hadn't had time to look at his phone to check, but they must have been moving for hours. They were tired, cold, wet, and wanted nothing more than to be back at home in their beds – asleep, warm, and waking up to find out that this was all a dream.

"Snap out of it!" Cindy said, punching Ben's shoulder.

"Ow! Again with the shoving and hitting," Ben responded.

"You were daydreaming," Cindy said, suddenly whispering. "Keep your voice down. I think we might have lost it."

"Why are we keeping our voices down if we lost it?" Ben asked.

"Brothers," Cindy muttered.

The kids had come to a small clearing in the forest. In the center, there was an enormous stump from a long-dead tree. It looked about the size of a small car. They noticed a hollow on one side of it – a hiding place? Finding the energy for one last sprint, Ben and Cindy raced for the hollow and nestled inside.

"Check your phone," Cindy said anxiously.

Ben was already ahead of her. He was on the

Tales to Astonish website, checking the thread he had started. He did a double take when he saw there was a response to his query about the statue. He did another double take when he saw who had left the message.

Kid Kaiju!

"What are you doing?" Cindy asked. "What are you looking at? Let me see!"

"Kid Kaiju! He posted to our thread! He says, 'That thing is called the Glop. You need to get away from it as fast as you can. The statue itself isn't the problem. It's that goo. It's a monster . . . from outer space!'"

CHAPTER 18

IT WASN'T LIKE creatures from outer space were anything new. Everyone at school had heard about the Guardians of the Galaxy, a team of Super Heroes whose members came from, well, across the galaxy. If there was a talking tree person and a wisecracking raccoon from space, why not a big globby monster?

"I would say I don't believe it, but after everything I've seen the last couple of days, it makes perfect sense," Cindy said.

"No kidding!" Ben replied, excited and scared at the same time. He kept reading Kid Kaiju's post.

KidKaiju:

I believe the goo is alien in origin. Based on my research, the alien needs to absorb something in order to grow and move. The goo, that glop that you're seeing around town, was somehow attracted to the statue in your town. It coated the statue, almost like paint. Now it can move at will. That's not good.

"You mean we were walking around town with alien goo all over our shoes?" Cindy said. "Yuck."

"Shhhh!" Ben said, agitated. "There's more!"

KidKaiju:

Checking on some of the details, but I can tell you this: according to notes written by Elsa Bloodstone, the first reported sighting of the Glop was more than thirty years ago, in Europe. One of my sources indicates the country was Transylvania (you know, Dracula country).

KidKaiju:

Apparently, some crazy scientist (is there any other kind?) had found some strange goo and an ancient parchment. He spent years trying to decipher the parchment. When he did, he discovered that the goo was actually a dormant alien. In order for the alien to "come back to life," it needed to absorb something large, something metal (not sure why). So the scientist hired an unsuspecting young artist to "paint" a statue with the substance.

"Elsa Bloodstone!" Ben exclaimed. "I read about her – she comes from a family of monster hunters! She's like, the numero uno head monster person!"

"Keep reading!" Cindy said, punching her brother on the arm.

KidKaiju:

The artist painted the statue, and as you probably guessed, the "statue" appeared to come to life. And it was hungry. So the goo absorbed it. And it grew.

KidKaiju:
And still it was hungry. It ate anything. Everything. Buildings. People. Pigs. There were probably pigs.

"Pigs?" Cindy said, raising an eyebrow. "That's random."

KidKaiju:
From everything I can gather, you have one chance to stop this thing. You have to find a way to dissolve the glop in order to stop the Glop!

"That seems easy!" Ben exclaimed. "Right? Pretty basic?"

Cindy rolled her eyes. "Ohhhh, yeah. Easy. We just have to figure out how to dissolve some alien life-form. Easy peasy, lemon squeezy."

"You say that like it's going to be hard," Ben said with a straight face. Both kids laughed.

Suddenly, a sound.

"Eaaaaaaasssssssyyyyyyyy peeaaassssssyyyy . . ."

Ben and Cindy whipped their heads up to look at the entrance of the hollow in the tree.

They saw nothing.

"Was that you?" Cindy asked.

Ben shook his head no.

Ben was going to suggest that maybe it was Cindy or the wind or one of a hundred other things, but it was pretty obvious that it wasn't any of them.

It became even more obvious when the tree trunk that had been their hiding place was suddenly uprooted from the ground, roots and all.

CHAPTER 19

"LLLLLLEEENMMMMOONNNNN

squeeeeeeezzzzzyyyyyy!!!"

The Glop had found them. With barely a thought, the creature tore the tree stump from its roots and tossed it aside like the bad test paper that Ben had crumpled up earlier that week because there was no need to keep a test on which he got a 39 out of 100.

Like a flash, they were on their feet and out of there. Ben and Cindy sprinted across the clearing, diving through the Glop's gloppy legs, landing at a stand of trees on the opposite side. The Glop turned, faster than you'd think, to face the kids. If it had a face, it looked almost like it was smiling.

Like it was playing some kind of sick, twisted game.

"It did NOT just say 'Easy peasy, lemon squeezy,'" Cindy gasped, as she grabbed her brother's sweatshirt, pulling him into the forest.

"I think it did," Ben said. "That might be scarier than anything else so far."

"It is *absolutely* scarier than anything else so far."

"Yooooooooooooouuuuuuuuu arrrrrrreeeeeee dooooooommmmeeeeed!" shrieked the Glop, its wet voice echoing through the clearing. Then it started to move, one gloppy "leg" after another. Faster. Faster. Closer. Closer.

"I don't wanna be doooooooommmmeeeeed!" Ben yelled.

Ben and Cindy ran as fast as they could.

o o o

"Do you have a signal yet?" Cindy asked, as twigs snapped beneath her feet. She ducked under a branch, narrowly avoiding a collision.

"Signal? What? Why? For whaaaaaaaah?" Ben said as he tripped and slid down a muddy incline on his back.

82

"Why? To call for help! The cops! The National Guard! The army! The Avengers! SOMEONE!" she said.

"Call and tell them WHAT?" Ben said, back up and running. "A giant pile of glop is gonna gobble us up? They'll never believe it! Don't you watch horror movies? Adults never believe the kids until it's too late!"

Ben thought for a second as he picked himself off the muddy ground.

"Well, the Avengers might believe it, maybe, but I don't exactly have their number in my contacts. Besides, aren't they off fighting the Masters of Evil or something?"

"Then what about Spider-Man? He's the friendly *neighborhood* Spider-Man – we *live* in a neighborhood . . . he should *have* to help!" Cindy said, practically hyperventilating.

"We also don't have Spider-Man's number in our contacts," Ben said.

No, Ben thought. *Calling for the cops isn't going to help.* It's not like Don Cyphers's dad would be able to do anything against that slime from space: *Now get home, Glop, before I call your parents!* Yeah, that wasn't gonna work.

But Kid Kaiju . . . now *he* might be able to help!

It wasn't easy, but Ben called up *Tales to Astonish* on his phone while he was running. The screen was bouncing up and down as Ben tried to look at it. His stomach felt a little queasy. He remembered that he had skipped dinner and hadn't really had anything to eat since lunch earlier that day.

"Hold on!" he called to Cindy, who had gotten ahead of him. She stopped, turned, and shot him a look.

"Hold on? We have to keep running! Did you see how fast the Glop was moving? It'll be here any second!"

Ben held up a finger as if to say, *Just give me a minute*. He typed on his phone as fast as he could. A bead of sweat from his forehead dripped onto the phone. He wiped it away.

Then another bead of sweat dripped.

Wipe.

And another.

Wipe. And another.

And it was then that Ben realized it wasn't sweat at all.

It was glop.

CHAPTER 20

KEI COULDN'T BELIEVE IT. He was glued to his computer, reading a new post from benthemonsterkid.

And it wasn't good.

benthemonsterkid:
The Glip us slivr! Qfter us! We r on th run nd ned helpk!

Kei read the message, his mouth agape. Aside from the typos, it was clear that the monster kid was in trouble! But what did "The Glip us slivr" mean? Kei figured that "Glip" was "Glop," but "slivr"? If the monster kid was on the run, that would account for all the mistyped letters. Kei glanced down at his keyboard and typed

SLIVR

He looked at his fingers on the keyboard. Then it hit him. *S* was right next to *A*. The *R* was right next to *E*.

benthemonsterkid hadn't typed "The Glip us slivr."

He had typed, "The Glop is alive!"

∘ ∘ ∘

In addition to the sloppy text message, benthemonsterkid had also told Kei where they were located. It was too far away for Kei himself to get there to help. Not in time, anyway. He needed someone who could get there fast. From watching the news with his mom, he knew that the Avengers were off fighting the Masters of Evil. So even if he could get in touch with them, they wouldn't be able to help.

But he didn't need the help of a Super Hero.

No, what Kei needed was the help of *another* monster. Something that could give the Glop a

fight and give Ben the monster kid a chance.

Now *that* was something that Kid Kaiju could handle!

CHAPTER 21

WHEN BEN LOOKED UP and over his shoulder, he saw what he thought was a huge tree in the shadows. Except this tree moved and was dripping wet.

Dripping with glop.

"Eaaaaassssssyyyyyy peeeaaaassssssyyyyyy . . ." the Glop hissed, spitting little drops of glop from its "mouth."

"Stop saying that!" Ben shouted. He started to run, then tripped, rolling down a hill. His sister grabbed his arm and pulled him to his feet.

"Run!" she shouted as the Glop smashed a tree in half with a gloppy appendage.

"Who told you to stop and text?" Cindy said,

angry. "I said CALL somebody! It's a phone, too, you know!"

"I did better than call somebody," Ben said, huffing and puffing. "I made a post to *Tales to Astonish*! I told Kid Kaiju where we were and what was happening! I told him that the Glop is alive!"

They had managed to put a little distance between themselves and the great gloppy beast that pursued them. Ben shoved his phone into Cindy's face, proudly showing her the message that he had sent to Kid Kaiju via *Tales to Astonish*. Cindy pushed the phone back at him and kept on running.

"Are you nuts? Why are you showing this to me now, when we need to be running!" she shouted. Then she added, "You wrote 'The Glip us slivr.'"

"I what?" Ben said, panting.

"You heard me. 'The Glip us slivr.' What does that even mean? Nice typos!"

As both kids ran past trees and branches, Cindy glared at Ben. "Let's hope Kid Kaiju can read your crazy message," she said to her brother.

"Hey," Ben replied. "You try texting while you're running from that thing!!"

o o o

"You've got to be kidding me," Cindy said, bent over and out of breath.

Ben was bent over, too, his head between his knees, trying to catch his own breath. His chest ached. His sides hurt. It felt like they had been running for hours. He didn't even know where they were anymore. Were they still in the woods?

"What is it?" Ben asked, without bothering to look up. His head felt like a bowling ball – almost too heavy for him to pick up. Besides, he didn't want to see anything else. Everything he had seen so far that night had been pretty terrible.

"You have to see it to believe it."

Sighing, Ben looked up. He and his sister had come to another clearing in the woods, and in the distance, they saw a beat-up, weathered old house. The exact kind of house that kids would say was haunted. Boards were missing, shutters were hanging off at the hinges. Ben could have sworn he saw a bat or two flying overhead in the moonlight, but that was probably just his imagination.

But do you know what wasn't his imagination?

The graveyard that stood between them and the house and beyond that, the woods on the other side of the clearing.

"A cemetery?! Why is there a cemetery in the middle of the woods?" Ben said. "Come ON! Like it isn't creepy enough, getting chased by the Glop. Now we have to run through a graveyard?"

"I know, right?" Cindy said in disbelief. "This is fifty kinds of unfair."

Cindy was right. Neither of them relished the thought of wandering through a remote graveyard in the dead of night. But they couldn't just stand there. They knew they had to keep moving if they were going to have a prayer of staying ahead of the Glop.

"Maybe we can go a different way," Cindy suggested. "Head back into the woods? Maybe it won't see us!"

"I don't know, Cindy," Ben said, still trying to

catch his breath. "We've been running forever. We have to find someplace to hide and rest. Even for just a little bit. Maybe that house . . . ?"

Cindy put her foot down. "I am *not* running through a graveyard."

There was a gurgling sound in the distance and the sound of twigs snapping.

"Or we could just cut through the graveyard and head for the abandoned house!" she said, sprinting ahead of her brother.

Ben followed. Both kids raced through the graveyard, passing by old, crumbling gravestones. The ground was a bumpy, pitted mess, littered with rocks. Ben almost fell a few times, and Cindy fared little better. But somehow they managed to make it through the creepy maze of graves and to the abandoned house beyond.

"Let's head inside," Ben said, walking up the clattering steps. "Maybe we can find a good hiding spot. Rest up before we have to start running from the Glop again."

Cindy looked up at the withered house, fully

expecting a mob of brain-hungry zombies to come crashing through each and every window. But it was this or get eaten by the Glop.

She took a big gulp, nodded, and followed her brother into the dark, foreboding house.

CHAPTER 22

IF THE KIDS THOUGHT that it might not be as creepy inside the old house as outside, they were wrong.

It was a million times *more* creepy.

The house was dark, save for the slivers of moonlight that came in through the broken windows and a few cracks in the walls. Through the shadows they could see small portions of the entry room, but not the whole place. They could make out an old, broken chair in the corner.

There was a weird *skritching* sound that echoed around the room.

"What was that?" Cindy whispered.

Ben shook his head and took a couple of

tentative steps inside. The floor beneath his feet moaned. He felt the rotting wood give a little.

There was the skritching sound again, as a rat emerged from the darkness and ran over Cindy's foot. To be fair, it was kind of a cute rat. But, you know, it was still a rat. Cindy jumped, but it was Ben who stifled a scream with his right hand.

"Oh, come on, it's just a rat," Cindy said. "And it ran over my foot, not yours."

"Sorry," Ben whispered back. "Sympathy scream."

Slowly, the kids crept inside the room, walking carefully on the rotting, creaking floor. They had to be careful to make as little noise as possible. The Glop wasn't far behind them and was sure to come across the house just like they had. If the creature heard noise coming from inside the house, it would be all over for them.

A few more steps in, and Ben spied some stairs that led to the second floor. "There!" he said in a hushed voice. "Up those stairs. Maybe the place has an attic where we can hide."

The kids made their way across the floor toward

the stairs. They were almost there. Ben took a step, setting his foot down on the floor.

Except the floor wasn't there!

As he was toppling over, he saw through the darkness. The entire floor in front of the stairs was missing! He could see into the cellar below, which was exactly where he was heading, face-first.

Until a hand grabbed his sweatshirt and yanked him backward. Hard.

Cindy held tight onto Ben, right at the edge of the big gap in the floor.

"Whoa! Thanks for the save!" Ben said. "Who did this? The rats?"

Cindy shook her head. "People. The wood floors in some of these old houses are worth a lot of money. Someone probably came in at night and stole the wood so they could sell it."

Ben looked at his sister and raised an eyebrow. "How do you know all that?"

She shrugged. "Sometimes I watch home-repair shows when you're busy drawing your monsters."

A gap of about ten feet separated Ben and Cindy

from the stairs. It was very clear they weren't going that way. On the other hand, they now had direct access to the cellar. They looked into the black void. They couldn't really see anything. All they could hear was more skritching. Rats.

"I hate to say it, but the basement is probably our best bet," Ben said. "You could lower me down there, and then you can jump – I'll catch you."

"That seems like a terrible plan," Cindy said. "Let's do it."

Ben moved toward the opening, when the skritching sound suddenly grew louder. Much louder. And closer.

There, in the darkness, they saw it – them.

Eyes.

Red rat eyes.

Hundreds of them.

And they were all heading directly toward Ben and Cindy!

CHAPTER 23

YOU KNOW WHAT STINKS? Being in a situation where you really, really want to scream, but you can't. Like when hundreds of rats come skittering at you in a dark, creepy old house. You want to yell as loud as you can. But Ben and Cindy couldn't scream. They couldn't afford to make a sound, otherwise the Glop would know exactly where they were.

They shouldn't have worried. They should have screamed as loud as they wanted to.

Because there was a reason the rats were suddenly running.

They weren't running at Ben and Cindy.

They were running *away* from something.

As the rats skittered past Ben and Cindy, the floorboards beneath them came to life. It was like someone took a rug, held it by two ends, and shook it. The floor rippled in a wave, throwing Ben and Cindy up into the air. They landed with a dull thud on the rotting wood. Ben's elbow went through a board.

They struggled to their feet. As they did, they saw something rising through the giant hole in the floorboards in front of the stairs. Something huge, something hulking.

Something gloppy.

"Eeeeeeasssssssssyyyyyyy peasssssssssyyyyy," said the Glop. Ben didn't know if that thing had any emotions, but it sure seemed happy to him. Like it was gloating. As if it knew that it had Ben and Cindy right where it wanted them.

The Glop was now fully formed in front of Ben and Cindy, taking up the entire hole in the floorboards. Hiding in the house was no longer an option. They had to get out of there, and fast. They turned tail and bolted for the front door where they had come in just a few minutes earlier.

The Glop shot out a gloppy hand, trying to shut the door before the kids could escape. Ben saw the hand from the corner of his eye. He did what anyone in his situation would do.

He pushed his sister.

"Hey!" Cindy shouted in protest, as Ben shoved her away from the door and toward a window right next to it. As both kids tumbled out of the empty window frame, the Glop's oozing hand slammed the door shut with such force that it not only pulverized the door, but it took the whole doorframe with it. A shower of splinters rained on the front porch.

Ben and Cindy rolled onto the muddy ground below the window. Inside they heard the Glop moving. Coming for them.

It was time to run.

CHAPTER 24

THEIR LEGS WERE DEAD TIRED, but somehow, they kept running. Had they been running all night? Ben glanced down at his phone.

4:30 a.m.

Ever since the encounter at the abandoned house, they had managed to evade the Glop. But sooner or later, they were going to have to stop running. And when they did, the Glop was sure to find them. It always seemed to find them.

"Any word from Kid Kaiju?" Cindy asked. It had been a while since Ben had checked *Tales to Astonish*.

Ben broke pace for just a second so he could grab his phone from his pocket. He loaded the *Tales to Astonish* thread. There was one new message from Kid Kaiju:

 KidKaiju:
I'm on it!

"Well?" Cindy asked again.

"He says, 'I'm on it,'" Ben replied. "That's – that's good, right?"

Cindy jumped over a rock in her path. "Yeah, that's great. Oh, did you remind him that a giant Glop is TRYING TO EAT US?!?"

"I think I might have already mentioned that, yeah," Ben shot back.

They kept running in silence.

• • •

"The school!" Ben said, breaking the quiet between them.

Cindy turned to look at her brother. Then, realizing what he meant, she peered through the trees before them. In the distance, she could see it.

Kurtzberg Middle School! If they could make it to the school – to shelter – they might have a chance! They could catch their breath, make a plan, and figure out a way to stop the Glop before it took over their town . . . and the world.

"That's perfect!" Cindy said, hope in her voice. "Plus, there's no creepy graveyard . . ."

". . . and no rats!" Ben finished.

With an end to the running in sight, the kids redoubled their efforts. They sprinted through the forest toward the edge. They tumbled down a hill and rolled right out of the trees into a grassy patch behind Kurtzberg Middle School.

They landed right in front of a huge, overpowering figure!

CHAPTER 25

"AAAAAAAAAAAHHHHHHHHH!!!"

Ben screamed, startling his sister, who started screaming, too.

They looked up at the "overpowering figure." In the darkness, Ben thought it was the Glop, looming over them. But it turned out to be a statue of the school's founder, Jacob Kurtzberg.

"Oh, man, I do not need more scares like that," Ben said. "I am *done* with statues."

Cindy punched her brother on the arm for what felt like the millionth time. "That's for scaring me for nothing," she said.

The ground rumbled.

"What was that?" Ben shouted.

Again the ground rumbled, and the statue of Jacob Kurtzberg trembled, then fell over! Beneath it, a gooey substance began to bubble up, growing, rising, until it formed the now familiar shape of . . .

The Glop!

"Wait, that thing can burrow under the ground, too?" Cindy yelled. "Not fair!"

The creature threw back its "head," and a stream of glop flew through the air as it did. It raised two massive appendages above its "head," like it was about to crush Ben and Cindy.

They closed their eyes. It seemed like the end. After everything, after all the running, after the escape from the old house, after meeting Kid Kaiju – well, exchanging message-board posts with Kid Kaiju! – it was over. Ben and Cindy were cornered by the Glop.

An unearthly sound filled the air. It was something they hadn't heard before, something unfamiliar.

Ben was just glad it wasn't the Glop saying *Easy peasy, lemon squeezy.*

A screech. Then wind. A wind so massive, it actually forced Ben flat on the ground. Cindy, too.

Then came a heavy, dull thud in front of them.

They opened their eyes and looked up from the ground. Standing in front of Ben and Cindy – between them and the Glop – enormous green scaly reptile with the weirdest wings either had ever seen.

Another monster.

The new monster looked at Ben and Cindy and sniffed. It was like a dog, checking the scents around it. The monster sniffed some more, then seemed to nod its large green head at the kids. It had big, wobbly, batlike ears that shook when it nodded.

Somehow, the kids knew that this new monster was not there to hurt them. No, he was there to protect them.

The Glop let out a sound that was so sickening, it almost made Ben throw up. It unleashed a torrent of glop at this new monster and the kids right behind it. Before either Ben or Cindy knew what was happening, the monster scooped them up in its huge, clawed, webbed-finger hands, and leaped into the sky! The stream of glop landed on the ground below them. Ben watched in horror as the goo rolled back toward the Glop. Was it his imagination, or did the Glop seem bigger than before?

The flying reptile monster set down Ben and Cindy close to the school entrance, then turned its attention back toward the Glop. It narrowed its eyes as it stared at the oozing horror, and then, without any warning, sprayed flames from its mouth! The flames engulfed the Glop, and it made a sound – something like a howl of pain? Ben wasn't sure if the fire hurt the Glop or not, but it definitely slowed it down . . .

Until goo from the Glop's body slid over the flames and extinguished them.

Ben glanced down at his phone as the two monsters circled each other. He saw a reply to his thread on *Tales to Astonish* – it was Kid Kaiju!

KidKaiju:
I sent someone to help. You're gonna need it. I couldn't come with or I would have slowed him down, but my friend should heat things up! His name is Slizzik, and he won't let you down.

"We have our own monster now?" Cindy whooped. "This is awesome!"

CHAPTER 26

"THIS IS NOT AWESOME!" Ben shouted, as a large glob of glop flew just inches from his head, landing on the bench the kids were using for cover. The gooey substance now seemed to dissolve the part of the bench that it hit. The goo swelled a bit, like it was absorbing the bench parts. Then the goo rolled back toward the Glop.

"I mean, it's awesome watching two giant monsters fight, but it's less awesome when the Glop tries to glop us!" Ben said, all in one breath.

Slizzik breathed another fiery blast at the Glop. Once again, the Glop recoiled from the flames, as the goo from its body rose to dampen them. It seemed like Slizzik's fire only slowed the slimy

creature, but couldn't really hurt it.

That's exactly what Ben was typing to Kid Kaiju at that moment. If he had sent Slizzik to help them, then Kid Kaiju should know that the plan wasn't working! Ben finished typing and hit the Post button. He hoped that Kid Kaiju was glued to *Tales to Astonish* and would respond quickly.

By now, it was obvious that the Glop was growing. It was much bigger than when it first came to life in the town square. Ben observed that over time, the Glop had become almost like an acid, dissolving everything it touched, making more goo.

The Glop seemed to know this, too, as it spewed more gross goo at Slizzik, who dodged the mess, moving incredibly fast for something his size. The great beast beat his wings rapidly. The wind generated by his wings pushed the Glop backward – not much, but a little bit. The Glop struggled against the wind.

"He wrote back!" Cindy hollered, and Ben pulled himself away from the monstrous battle to check his phone.

KidKaiju:

That's a problem! So it seems the Glop might not exactly be immune to fire, but it doesn't really hurt it, either. Slizzik should be able to keep the Glop busy. But you're going to have to find a way to beat it! I'll do what I can from my end. . . .

Ben and Cindy looked at each other. They turned their heads and looked at Slizzik, flapping its huge wings. They saw the Glop slowly advancing against the wind toward Slizzik.

"How," Ben said incredulously, "are we gonna stop THAT?"

CHAPTER 27

BEN TRIED TO WRAP his brain around everything that was happening. All he and his sister had to do was figure out a way to stop a gross, sticky alien from outer space.

Piece of cake.

"You're coming up with a plan, right?"

Cindy's voice snapped Ben out of his thoughts. It took a second or two to register what she had said.

"Um, yeah, a plan, of course!" he said. The words were hardly out of his mouth when the Glop sprayed more of his disgusting ooze at Slizzik. The winged reptile was doing its best to draw the Glop's "fire" away from the kids, but the monstrosity was losing interest in battling the fire-breathing lizard. It was not, however, losing interest in getting Ben and Cindy.

"Doooo nooooot resssssisssst ussssssss!" the Glop hissed. "Weeeeee wiilllllll abbbbssssssooooorrrrbbbb youuuuuuuu . . . youuuuuuuu wwwwwiiiiiillllllll beeeeeeecommmmmeeeee ussssss!"

So that was the Glop's gross plan? It was going to attack Ben and Cindy and then add them to its slimy body?

"Oh, no," Cindy said, shaking her head. "Oh, heck no!"

Ben should have been so afraid that he couldn't move – an alien from another world just threatened to absorb him and his sister into its oozy body! But he was too busy trying to figure out a way to escape from the Glop. The answer was right in front of him. The school. They had to get inside the school.

"Hey, Glop!" Ben yelled as he stood up, waving both arms wildly. The sound and motion immediately caught the creature's attention, and its "head" wrenched around 180 degrees, staring at him.

Cindy looked at her brother like he was out of his mind. "I'm sorry, you WANT him to come after us?"

"Yeah, I do! Come on, Glop! Bet you can't hit us!" Cindy now realized what her brother was doing. Ben was taunting the creature. The Glop let out a sound – was it an evil laugh? – then his spat its horrible goo right at Ben and Cindy. Ben grabbed his sister's arm and pulled her down to the ground with him.

The goo missed by inches but completely nailed the side of the school. Within moments, the goo dissolved the brick exterior, making an enormous hole in the school wall. The goo grew even bigger. The strange substance rolled back toward the Glop and became part of its body – making the Glop even larger than before.

Cindy stood, gaping at the Glop in disbelief. "Wait, now he can *dissolve* stuff? NO. WAY!"

"Maybe it's evolving," Ben guessed. "Remember what Kid Kaiju said? How the Glop started to eat everything in sight?"

As if in answer, the Glop covered a nearby playground slide in goo. The slide melted away as it was dissolved and absorbed into the goo.

"Inside, now!" Ben shouted, shoving his sister toward the opening in the school that the Glop had made.

The creature was furious. Only then did it realize that it had been tricked. It moved with tremendous speed toward the hole in the wall. Slizzik was behind it and tried to prevent the Glop from entering. But the flying reptile was too late! The Glop oozed through the hole.

Slizzik tried to enter, but its huge wingspan prevented it from going inside the school.

That left Ben and Cindy inside Kurtzberg Middle School all alone.

With the Glop.

CHAPTER 28

IT WAS 5:00 A.M., prime monster time. It wasn't uncommon for Kei to be awake at that hour. It was quiet, and there was no one to bother him as he devoured information from *Tales to Astonish* and sketched his monsters.

But this morning was different from those quiet ones. Sure, Kei was wide-awake at 5:00 a.m., but it wasn't to pursue his passions. Not for fun, anyway. It was because he was worried about benthemonsterkid! It was clear now that Slizzik's fire alone wasn't going to be able to stop the Glop.

So what would stop it? Was there another monster at Kei's fingertips that could send the Glop packing?

He needed a plan.

He went back to *Tales to Astonish*, to the Monster Lore tab, and reread the article on the Glop. Maybe there was something in Elsa Bloodstone's notes that would help them.

And then he came across something in Elsa's notes, something that he hadn't noticed before:

". . . *discovered the diary of a man who claimed to have fought the Glop many years ago. He wrote, 'I waited tensely until the pursuing Glop was within range . . . then I hurled the open can straight at him! Immediately the thick bubbling "paint" began to dissolve. . . .'"*

So there was a way to stop it!

"Wait . . . an open can of WHAT?" Kei said, scratching his head. He checked the entry and read through Elsa Bloodstone's notes. There was no mention of what exactly the man had used to stop the Glop. Now his mind moved from thoughts of monsters to solving this problem.

What could have dissolved the Glop?

CHAPTER 29

IT WAS DARK inside the school, save for the dull red light emanating from the Exit signs. Ben and Cindy had never been inside Kurtzberg Middle School at night, let alone all by themselves. It was a small town, a small school, and there was no security guard after hours. There was no alarm ringing, either. Ben wondered why, then realized – the alarms were probably programmed to trip if a door or window was opened. But not if some gigantic Glop dissolved a hole in the wall!

The kids padded down the hallway, racing past the closed, darkened classrooms. They looked over their shoulders. In the dark, they saw nothing but lockers lining either side of the hallway. Then they heard a distant sound – like enormous flapping wings.

"He's still outside," said Cindy.

"Who? Slizzik, or the Glop?"

"Slizzik. You hear the wings?"

"Yeah," Ben said. "So where's the Glop?"

As if on cue, there came a gurgling sound. Like a low rumble. The kids could feel the vibrations through their shoes, running up their legs.

"What is *that*?" Cindy asked. "Do you see anything?"

Ben rubbed his tired eyes and squinted. His vision had adjusted somewhat to the low-level lighting in the school. But when he looked down the hallway, he still saw nothing. He turned and looked behind them. Nothing.

No sign of the Glop anywhere.

"Nothing!" Ben said nervously.

They kept walking, looking for a good place to hide.

Again, the floor rumbled beneath them. They heard a "shlorp" sound, like someone flinging a blob of gelatin at a wall.

A locker door jangled. Cindy whipped her head around to look at the row of lockers right next to her.

One of the doors was ajar. Cindy gulped.

"There!" she whispered, pointing at the open locker door. Ben nodded. Summoning all the courage he had inside, he crept over to the locker door and looked at his sister. She gave him a look that said, *What are you doing?!* Ben nudged his head toward the locker door, then looked at his foot and wiggled it. Then he pretended to kick the door. Cindy nodded, getting it.

She held her breath.

With a loud clang, Ben kicked open the locker door.

A stack of books and a brown paper bag fell out of the locker and onto the floor. The paper bag came to rest on its side, and an apple rolled out.

Cindy exhaled, and Ben slumped against the row of lockers.

"I'd like to go home now," Cindy said.

"I'd like that apple," Ben said. "I haven't had anything to eat since forever."

That's when the locker doors on the opposite side of the hallway blew wide open, the Glop flowing freely from every single opening.

CHAPTER 30

"**WHAT THE GLOP!**" Ben yelled, as he and Cindy motored down the hallway. The Glop was no longer walking upright, like a grim parody of a person. It was now flowing, like a river of sick and disgusting slop. It rolled and roiled behind the kids, chasing after them. It moved along the floor, to the lockers, over the ceiling, to the other side of the hall, back to the floor, always going forward. It crested in waves, an ocean of slime heading closer and closer toward Ben and Cindy.

As the kids turned the corner, they saw that the

hall dead-ended. In front of them was the school gym.

"Inside!" Cindy said, grabbing her big brother. They pushed the doors open and ran into the gym. Their sneakers squeaked across the floor. Behind them, the Glop gurgled and flowed quickly toward them.

"Nnnnoooooooo esssssscaaaaaaaaappe" were the words that bubbled from its "mouth."

Inside the gym, Ben looked around for anything they might use to slow down the Glop. He saw a balance beam the students used for gymnastics lessons and had an idea.

"Grab the other end of this!" he said to his sister, and the two pushed the balance beam over to the doors that led inside the gym. Since the doors were the kind you pushed, Ben figured if they could block the door with the balance beam, they could prevent the Glop from opening the door!

The creature threw itself against the double doors, now blocked by the balance beam. They didn't open!

"Score one for the good guys!" Ben said, a little triumph in his voice.

Which is when the doors slowly began to dissolve. The large Glop oozed through the now open doorway and into the gym.

"So much for that bright idea," Ben said, as the kids raced across the gym floor. All they had to do was make it to the door on the opposite side of the gym to escape the Glop.

They ran as fast as they could, but somehow the Glop was faster, always faster. It spread itself like an oil slick across the gym floor, causing the kids to slip and slide on the hardwood.

Ben and Cindy picked themselves up as the Glop continued to slime its way across the gym floor. They were only about twenty feet from the door. But between them and the door now stood the Glop. It had oozed back into its hulking, walking form.

"We're not getting out that way," Ben said, his heart pounding. He looked around, his mind reeling.

"What are we gonna do?" Cindy said. "If we try

to run back to the other doors, it's just gonna trip us up again! And then what? Eat us?"

Ben craned his neck, scanning the gym for some other way out. That's when his eyes noticed the climbing wall.

And the air vent above it.

"Climb the wall, NOW!" Ben yelled to his sister, as he ran for the other doors.

CHAPTER 31

BEN WAVED HIS ARMS and whooped and hollered as he ran toward the other doors. If the Glop had any emotions, it was probably all too happy to follow him. It seemed attracted to all the commotion he was making.

And it seemed hungry.

"Over here, Sloppy Joe!" he taunted. The creature complied, sliding and slipping along the gym floor, leaving gloppy splotches along the way. The thing seemed to pay no attention to Cindy, as she made it to the climbing wall.

And she climbed.

Fast.

Ben was nearly at the other doors when the

Glop suddenly flowed up and around the doors themselves. It blocked the exit, burbling and bubbling at Ben. He looked behind him and saw Cindy climbing. She was nearly at the top of the rock wall, near the vent!

Cindy saw her brother bravely confronting the Glop. She was so proud of her brother . . . but she would never tell him that! *I'll never hear the end of it*, she thought. Ben had bought them time to escape from the gym, given her a chance to get to the vent. Maybe they'd be able to escape through it and crawl to safety.

Now it was her turn to help her brother. She made it to the top of the rock wall, to the air vent, grabbed the grate that covered it with a free hand, and gave it a hard yank.

It barely budged.

"Whatever you're doing," Ben yelled to his sister, "can you do it faster?"

The Glop spat out a massive glob of goo at Ben, who managed to duck out of its way. The slime plopped onto the gym floor, dissolving a giant hole in the wooden planks. That blob grew bigger as it absorbed the wood, then rolled back to join the Glop . . . who seemed even larger.

Cindy pulled on the grate even harder, but it just wouldn't move. She looked at it again and saw that it had been painted over. Hundreds of times, it looked like. She doubted anyone this side of the Hulk could yank it off.

That's when it hit her.

"Hey!" Cindy called down below. "Glop! You're gross! And you smell! A lot!"

Ben's eyes went wide with terror for his sister. She was actually calling it over to her! What was she thinking?!

"Cindy, no!" Ben screamed, as the Glop forgot all about him. It reared its ugly, amorphous "head" and spat another wad of sticky, gloppy goo . . .

Right at Cindy!

CHAPTER 32

THERE WAS NOTHING Ben could do. It was too late. The Glop had gone after his sister, and there she was, hanging at the top of the climbing wall – helpless! The stream of slime seemed to take forever to arc through the air. Ben felt like he was moving in slow motion as he sprinted across the gym floor. He knew there was no way he could reach his sister before the Glop got to her. But he had to try.

He never took his eyes off Cindy. The Glop was almost upon her when she did something Ben didn't expect.

She let go of the climbing wall!

Cindy dropped a few feet before she managed

to catch another set of handholds. She looked up, just in time to see the Glop splatter right where she had just been . . .

Covering the air vent!

Down below, the Glop let out a garbled sound, as if it were angry, almost frustrated. *Sure*, Ben thought. *Of course it's frustrated. It's hungry and the two things it wants to eat the most keep running away!* Ben stared at the Glop on the wall as it dissolved the grate that covered the vent and dropped back down to the floor to join its master, narrowly missing Cindy on the way down.

Ben was now at the climbing wall, heading up to join his sister. He hadn't stopped running, hadn't stopped moving. He couldn't. They couldn't. Cindy had tricked the Glop into opening the blocked air vent for them! They had to make it through now. They had to!

By the time Ben reached the top of the climbing wall, Cindy had already clambered inside the air vent.

"Come on, give me your hand!" Cindy shouted,

and she helped pull Ben up and inside the vent. Below, they heard the ominous gurgling as the Glop dissolved more of the gym in a fit of anger. Now that Ben was safe inside the vent, both he and Cindy looked down. They saw the creature "eating" the bleachers and the floor, growing larger. It looked up at them.

"Ssssssssooooooon wwweeeee willlll eeeeeaaaat yyyooooou . . . annnndddd yoooouuuuuu wwwwilllll joooooooooiiiiinnnnnnn ussssssssss!"

CHAPTER 33

KEI'S FINGERS FLEW across the computer keyboard. Every other letter he pressed was wrong, and he found himself typing a message that read even worse than the one written by benthemonsterkid.

KidKaiju:
Pwint tjinner! I tink pint thiner wikk diffolve teh glip

Kei looked at what he had written, shook his head, and took a deep breath. He hit Delete, then retyped the message slowly, more carefully:

KidKaiju:
Paint thinner! I think paint thinner will dissolve the Glop!

He pressed Return to post the message to the thread.

Then he crossed his fingers for good luck. At times like these, Kei wished that Slizzik could talk, or that he was telepathic or something. It would be awesome to have a way of really communicating with him. *Moon Girl is lucky*, he thought. When she had to, she could somehow transfer her mind into the body of Devil Dinosaur, her companion. If Kei could have done that, he would "be" Slizzik, and would be helping benthemonsterkid right now!

But as it was, all he could do was wait. Kid Kaiju hoped that the monster kid would get this message, and that he'd be able to do something with the information.

Before it was too late.

CHAPTER 34

"THIS WAY!" Cindy called as she moved along the cramped air duct on her hands and knees. Ben was right behind her. He couldn't help glancing over his shoulder every other second or so, looking for any signs that the Glop was catching up to them.

So far, no sign. No nothing.

Was that good?

Or was it bad?

"We have to get out of the air duct, Cindy – we have to find a way out of here and the school, get back to Slizzik! We have to get back in touch with Kid Kaiju!"

They crawled down the air duct, not knowing exactly where they were. Finally, they came upon another vent and looked through the grate that covered it.

They saw the cafeteria.

"If the Glop makes it to the cafeteria, we'll never find it," Ben said, serious.

"What do you mean?" Cindy asked.

"I mean it's going to blend right in with all the gross cafeteria food," he replied.

Both kids laughed.

"Wait!" Ben exclaimed, as the phone in his pocket buzzed. He checked it and saw an update from Kid Kaiju. His eyeballs darted back and forth as he scanned the message. "For real, I know where we are and where we need to go! We have to make it to the next air vent!"

"What's the next air vent?" Cindy asked, as Ben squirmed around her and crawled faster and faster down the duct. "Where are we going?"

"The art room!" Ben yelled behind him.

"Aaaaaaaand why are we going to the art room?" Cindy asked. "Maybe we could make a prison for it out of macaroni and shells?"

"One more kick oughtta do it," Ben said. Both he and Cindy were all bent up inside the air duct, their backs against one side and their feet pressed against the grate covering the vent before them.

"One . . . two . . . THREE!" Ben called as he and Cindy slammed the soles of their feet against the grate. It came off and landed on the floor with a loud CLANG! They looked through the now open vent and saw the darkened art room. The vent was right above Mr. Pierce's desk.

Ben slipped out of the vent and landed on the desk. He looked up, and his sister jumped out, landing on her feet atop the desk.

"That was pretty cool, what you did back there in the gym," Ben had to admit.

Cindy smiled at her big brother. "Thanks. I guess it was pretty cool how you almost sacrificed yourself for me. So now what?"

"Kid Kaiju! His last post. Remember how he said that the stuff covering the Glop was like paint?"

Cindy nodded.

"Well, if it's like paint, then he said we need

something like paint thinner. You know, something that can dissolve paint! Maybe that's the Glop's weakness!"

"Maybe?" Cindy said.

"'Maybe' is better than 'We have no plan whatsoever except to become the Glop's next meal,'" Ben replied.

The kids looked at each other and nodded. The idea was far-fetched, but no more far-fetched than a giant, gloppy alien blob chasing them all over town and through their school. What did they have to lose by trying?

In the dark art room, Ben and Cindy went to the sink and the cabinets beneath it. There, among various empty bottles and paint cans, they found several jars marked PAINT THINNER. They started grabbing at them.

Then they heard a gurgling sound.

"Was that your stomach? Please tell me that was your stomach," Cindy said, remembering how hungry her brother was.

"It was not my stomach," Ben shot back.

Again, they heard the same gurgling sound. A second later, a stream of sickening goo erupted from the sink!

CHAPTER 35

THE GLOP EXPLODED from the sink, and Ben and Cindy fell to the floor. They looked up and saw the creature's disgusting form roll along the ceiling before landing on the floor and taking shape inside the art room. It looked bigger than ever! As it rose up on its two "legs," the Glop hunched over – it had to, in order to fit inside the room!

The kids were so distracted by the creature's sudden appearance that neither noticed they had let go of the jars of paint thinner. They rolled along the floor, coming to rest against a nearby sculpture.

"Nnnnnooooowwwwwwhheeerrrrrre tooooooo rrrrrrunnnnnnn," the Glop spat, tiny flecks of goo flying from its "mouth." The drops landed on the floor, dissolving little holes in its surface.

With surprising speed, the Glop reached for Ben. He tried to leap out of the way, when he saw the alien's other hand block his path.

"This is a terrible time to realize I dropped the paint thinner!" Ben shouted, probably to Cindy, but really to no one in particular.

Ben was cornered. The Glop was right – there was nowhere left to run! He was caught between the Glop's two massive hands, which were coming closer . . . and closer . . . and closer. . . .

CHAPTER 36

"INCOMING!"

Cindy.

Ben heard her voice and looked up. A big jar of paint thinner was flying through the air, right toward him. He shot up his hands and snagged it.

Right before the Glop's third hand slammed on top of its other two hands, effectively trapping Ben inside.

"Wait!" Ben cried. "Now it has THREE hands? I don't have three hands. This is *so* not fair!"

But that didn't matter. What mattered was that Ben had a jar of paint thinner. He was trapped by the Glop, but at least he had a chance to defend himself.

Maybe. After all, the paint thinner was only a theory, and an untested one at that. But there was no time like the present. Ben could hear all kinds of commotion from outside the walls of his gloppy prison. It sounded like the thing was going after Cindy now! He could hear his sister running from one side of the room to the other. At least, that's what it sounded like.

That's when he heard a splash and a scream!

But it wasn't Cindy screaming.

It was the Glop!

"Ben!" Cindy yelled, her voice muffled by the sound of the Glop's multiple "hands." "The paint thinner – it works!"

Ben quickly opened the jar, removing the lid. Then he splashed the contents of the open container at the "hand" that was closing in right in front of him.

The Glop shrieked in pain!

Almost immediately, the "hand" that had been hit by the paint thinner seemed to dissolve. The goo flowed away, creating an opening large enough for Ben to dive through, which is exactly what he did.

He was free!

Well, free from the gloppy prison. But still stuck inside the art room with a giant gloppy Glop!

Ben saw Cindy standing on the opposite side of the room, hurling the last of the paint thinner jars at the Glop. Wherever the paint thinner struck the creature's body, they saw the goo flowing away, like it was running from the chemical. Or like it was being dissolved? Gloppy goo from the creature's body flowed to cover these wounds, struggling to make the Glop whole again.

The Glop screamed. The paint thinner definitely hurt the alien. The creature shuddered, its massive form shaking as it rose.

Ben and Cindy's plan worked!

Which was good!

Except they were now out of paint thinner!

Which was bad!

Cindy and Ben took one look at each other, and without saying a word, raced for the windows. They opened one and crawled out while the Glop remained behind, recovering from the kids' attack.

They landed on the ground right beneath the window – it was a good thing the school had only one floor! The kids turned, and started to run . . .

Until they ran right into it.

CHAPTER 37

"IT" WAS SLIZZIK! Kid Kaiju's monster hadn't left. It had waited for the kids, as if it knew its help was still needed. The huge reptile bent down, then motioned with its huge head toward its back.

"I think it wants us to get on!" Ben said, climbing on top of Slizzik.

"Are we really gonna go for a ride on a flying whatsit?" Cindy asked.

SHLORP!

The art-room wall suddenly dissolved and was gone, as the Glop absorbed it into its body. The creature had recovered from Ben and Cindy's initial attack. It shambled through the large opening and

into the night, coming closer and closer to Slizzik, Ben, and Cindy.

Without another word, Cindy climbed on, followed by Ben.

"This is fine," Cindy said.

With a loud *whoosh*, Slizzik flapped its leathery wings, and the three were airborne. Below, the Glop stretched and distorted itself, trying to reach up into the sky to grab Ben and Cindy. But the kids' paint-thinner attack must have really hurt it – it let out an ear-piercing shriek and recoiled back in on itself.

Slizzik's wings flapped as they flew away from the school.

Below them, the Glop seethed.

And it began to follow.

● ● ●

Kei laughed at the fact that he was the only kid from his school who was awake at this hour, trying to find a way to help a couple of kids defeat a giant alien made of gross, living glop.

Kid Kaiju yawned and checked the *Tales to Astonish* message board. He hoped there would be an update from Ben. He hadn't heard anything from him in a while. Had Slizzik been able to help? And was Ben able to figure out a way to stop the runaway monster?

There was nothing Kei loved more than monsters, but they were becoming a big problem. He laughed at his own joke – "monsters," "big problem." He was doing everything he could to help anyone who ran into a monster problem. But he couldn't be everywhere at once.

● ● ●

"We can't keep running," Cindy said, hanging on to Slizzik's back. "Slizzik is great for a rescue, but even *he* can't hurt the Glop. What are we gonna do?"

Ben remained silent. Whenever he was quiet like this, Cindy knew that meant he was coming up with a plan. Sure, usually that plan involved him pranking her. But if he was using his "evil" powers against the Glop, who was she to judge?

"Mount Minor!" Ben blurted out.

"Mount Minor?" Cindy shot back. "You mean that dinky little hill? What's on Mount Minor?"

"Mr. Pierce!" Ben replied.

"The art teacher? The really, really old art teacher? The really, really, REALLY old art teacher?" Cindy asked. "How is he gonna help us?"

"I think he knows something about the Glop! When I showed him a picture of the statue the other day, he acted like he knew something about it. Like he had seen a moving statue before! Besides, even if he doesn't, he's an artist! He lives on Mount Minor, all by himself. And what does he like to do?"

Cindy shrugged her shoulders. "I don't know, what, paint?"

Paint.

Because where there was paint, there was . . .

"Paint thinner!" Cindy exclaimed.

Ben smiled and nodded. From their vantage point, Ben could see almost the whole town from above. Even in the darkness, Ben could see Mount Minor. After all, it was the tallest point in town. Again, not saying much, but still. He patted Slizzik on the head and pointed in its direction. Slizzik seemed to know exactly what that meant and

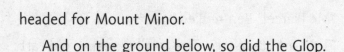

headed for Mount Minor.

And on the ground below, so did the Glop.

CHAPTER 38

BEN MANAGED a glance at his phone as Slizzik came in for a landing atop Mount Minor. It was 6:00 a.m. The sun would be coming up soon.

Had he and Cindy really been running from the Glop all night?

Slizzik's clawed feet touched down on the green grass of Mount Minor. It was a surprisingly soft landing. Slizzik bent down, making it easy for Ben and Cindy to climb off. Their feet planted firmly on the ground, they looked at Slizzik. The reptile stared back, and if Ben didn't know any better, he could have sworn that the corners of Slizzik's mouth rose slightly. Was that a smile?

"Hey, you kids!" came a voice from a tiny

ramshackle house about a hundred or so yards away. "Get off my lawn!"

It was Mr. Pierce.

He was dressed from head to toe in a dark green dressing robe and an old-fashioned sleeping cap. His glasses were perched atop his nose, and he cast his familiar sneer as he walked closer to them. All in all, Mr. Pierce looked like he had stepped right out of a Charles Dickens novel. That, or he could have been the headmaster at an exclusive school for witchcraft and wizardry.

"Mr. Pierce!" Ben said quickly. "I know this looks weird. . . ." He gestured toward Slizzik. "Understatement. And I know it's, like, six thirty in the morning! But we need your help!"

Mr. Pierce dismissively waved a hand at Ben. "Aaaaah, save it," he said, taking out his teeth and putting them back in. "I figured one of you kids would show up here sooner or later."

"Really? With a flying lizard, too?" Cindy asked, somewhat sarcastically.

"Let's just say it doesn't surprise me," Mr. Pierce

said. "At least it's not trying to burn my face off."

"Look, Mr. Pierce, we don't have time to explain," Ben said, trying to explain anyway. "But – "

That's when Mr. Pierce turned his back and headed toward his house. He held up a hand. "Aaaaah, save it," he said, which must have been one of his favorite things to say. "Everything old is new again."

"But, Mr. Pierce!" Ben called, but by then, the old art teacher had gone back inside his house.

In the distance, Ben and Cindy heard a gurgling, rumbling sound.

They knew what it was.

They knew *who* it was.

They knew it was coming closer.

It was a matter of time before the Glop arrived. And without paint thinner, without anything to stop the Glop, they would all be doomed.

"Ben, that hot mess is going to be here in just a minute!" Cindy said nervously. "And we're just standing outside the house of a creepy art teacher who plays with his false teeth!"

Those facts weren't lost on Ben. Had he been wrong? Maybe coming to Mount Minor to get Mr. Pierce's help was a mistake.

"Here, grab one o' these," said Mr. Pierce as he came back through the front door of his house. He was holding what looked like three large squirt-gun rifles, like the kind Ben and his sister would use to chase each other around the yard. Each rifle had a big cylinder connected to it, full of some kind of liquid.

There was another loud, gurgling rumble.

Shambling up to the top of Mount Minor was the familiar, gooey shape of the Glop.

"I said, take it!" Mr. Pierce ordered and shoved the squirt rifles at Ben and Cindy. They took them in hand.

"Now FIRE! Like your life depends on it!" yelled Mr. Pierce, taking aim.

CHAPTER 39

AND THEY DID! Ben, Cindy, and Mr. Pierce, squirt rifles in hand, blasted the Glop with streams of liquid. The towering Glop advanced, and Slizzik let loose another fire blast to keep the creature at bay while the others attacked.

The streams hit the Glop. At first, nothing seemed to happen. The Glop moved closer and closer.

And then . . .

The Glop screamed.

Ben and Cindy gasped as they watched glop fall away from the Glop! Everywhere they hit the creature, the gloppy goo seemed to dissolve away, to evaporate, just like in the art room.

"Paint thinner!" Ben shouted.

"Paint thinner!" Mr. Pierce replied.

They continued blasting the Glop all over its "body." The Glop continued to scream. Where it had been advancing, seemingly unstoppable, about to crush everyone, the Glop now tried to get away from the trio. It shifted its bulky "arms" as it tried to protect itself from the constant bursts of paint thinner.

The more the trio sprayed the Glop, the smaller he seemed to become!

Slizzik took to the air and flew around so it was facing the retreating Glop. It opened its mouth, drew in a breath, and then breathed fire toward the ground. It made a circle of flame all around the creature, Ben, Cindy, and Mr. Pierce. It was trapping the Glop inside the fiery circle with a bunch of paint-thinner-blasting heroes.

The Glop lifted its still-enormous "hands," trying to shield itself from the blasts of paint thinner. But it did little good. The gooey glop was dissolving. All over its body, the Glop was helpless but to watch the goo dissolve. There were huge holes now, holes the Glop couldn't begin to mend. The Glop seemed even smaller and struggled to walk away, toward the fire.

"Nnnoooooooooo!" it said, its voice growing weaker and weaker. "Mmmmuuusssssstttttt ggeeettttt awaaaayyyy . . . caannnnoooottttt endddddddd likkeeeeeeee . . . thisssssss!"

"Hit it in the legs or whatever you wanna call 'em!" yelled Mr. Pierce. Ben and Cindy took aim, and squirted the Glop's "legs." The goo dissolved away, leaving a much smaller blob of disgusting ooze sitting on the grass atop Mount Minor.

"This is for that thing that happened, and you know exactly what I'm talking about!" Mr. Pierce shouted and unloaded the rest of his paint thinner on the Glop. The kids followed suit.

In a matter of seconds, a once-titanic threat to the town had been completely dissolved. There remained no trace of the Glop. The smell of paint thinner filled the air, the only reminder of the monster's presence.

"How did you – how did you know?!" asked Ben in disbelief.

Mr. Pierce looked at the pool of paint thinner on the grass. "Kid, if you live long enough, you see everything."

The art teacher looked at Ben and Cindy, and he cracked a smile.

CHAPTER 40

THE SUN WAS just starting to come up. The day had arrived, and with it, the promise of a world free of glop and free *from* the Glop. By the time Ben, Cindy, and Mr. Pierce had exhausted their supply of paint thinner, the very last of the Glop had been dissolved. The air was pungent with paint thinner.

The fiery circle created by Slizzik had just about burned itself out. Mr. Pierce walked up to his house, dragged over a garden hose, and started to spray the smoldering ground with water.

"Safety first," he said, chuckling to himself. "Safety saves sickness, suffering, and sadness. Friend o' mine used to tell me that."

"I don't get it," Ben said, scratching his head. "Like, how?"

"Me either," Cindy added. "How did you know about the Glop, Mr. Pierce? How did you know what would stop him? How did you know we'd be coming to see you?"

"Why don't you kids ask as many questions when you're in my class? You'd all be geniuses!" Mr. Pierce replied. He waved them off with a hand. "I got hired to paint a statue with some kind of glop once. Thirty years ago. In Transylvania. Weird place. Let's just say I already lived through this. When everything started up in town, I tried to pretend it wasn't happening. Guess I should have been helping you kids all along."

"But – " Ben started, as Mr. Pierce waved him off again.

"Less you know the better!" he said. "Son, you're going to find in this world that there are some things you're just better off not knowing about. This is one of those things. Now get outta my yard! And take yer crazy flyin' lizard with you!" The fire was now out, and Mr. Pierce headed back to his house. He turned around to face the kids one last time.

"Oh, and school's canceled today. But you probably already figured that," he said, laughing.

CHAPTER 41

THEY STARTED DOWN the hill, back toward town. For a little while, Slizzik walked along with them, his head bobbing. The kids had grown used to their fiery friend, but they knew he had to leave. Ben grabbed his phone and called up *Tales to Astonish*. He responded to Kid Kaiju's last message.

benthemonsterkid:
The Glop is gone! Paint thinner did the trick. No more glop, no more Glop! Thanks for your help – and for lending us Slizzik! We're going to miss him.

Ben and Cindy turned to Slizzik, who bent his head down. Both gave him a little pat, and Slizzik snorted. He then lifted his head and started to back away. He flapped his great wings and, within seconds, was aloft. He rose into the sky and flew off into the dawn.

"Too bad he couldn't stay," Cindy said. "Could you imagine the look on Don Cyphers's face if he ever saw Slizzik?"

Ben laughed and looked at his phone. Kid Kaiju had responded!

◦ ◦ ◦

Kid Kaiju sat at his computer, smiling in relief. He'd just finished reading Ben's message – the Glop had been destroyed! He typed away on his keyboard.

KidKaiju:
Awesome!

KidKaiju:
Wish I could have been there in person to help. But I'm glad Slizzik was there. He's the best. I owe you one. The world owes you one! If you ever need help again, just say the word. Kid Kaiju will be there! Or at least Slizzik will! See you on *Tales to Astonish*!

Pushing himself away from the computer, Kid Kaiju leaned back in his chair. He was thrilled that Ben and his town were now safe. *Safety first*, Kei thought to himself. Just like his dad always said – "Safety first. Safety saves sickness, suffering, and sadness."

The threat of the Glop was over. But there were more monsters out there. There were more kids like Ben and Cindy who were going to need his help. He knew he couldn't be everywhere at once, so it was important that his helpers – good monsters, like Slizzik – were ready and raring to go.

"Monster trouble," Kid Kaiju said to himself, softly. He turned to his desk and his drawing pad. He had sketched out the rough form of a huge, gorillalike creature with a tail.

"Kei, breakfast is on the table!" called his mom from downstairs. "I know you're awake! Come down and eat, honey!"

Monsters will have to wait a minute, Kid Kaiju thought.

But only for a minute.

CHAPTER 42

BY THE TIME Ben and Cindy reached the town square, it was alive with excitement. It seemed like half the town, maybe the whole town, had turned out. *The statue is gone – of course it's gone,* Ben thought. He knew exactly where it went, too! It was eaten by an alien goo that had been dissolved in a shower of paint thinner atop Mount Minor.

The gloppy trail that had been left behind by the Glop had now dried up. Ben guessed that when the kids and Mr. Pierce put an end to the Glop (and the glop) atop Mount Minor, without a big host body to roll back to, the remaining glop had nowhere to go.

Sheriff Cyphers stood in the spot where the statue had been and tipped back his hat. He rubbed his forehead, confused.

"Ben, Cindy," he said, pointing his chin at them. "I see you came out along with the rest of the town to see what's going on. Well, it's nothing. Just a bunch of kids."

"You always say it's kids," came a voice from behind.

Don.

Sheriff Cyphers shrugged. "Well, all they did was steal a statue of Parka Guy, and leave a bunch of dried-up paint or whatever everywhere. Now who do you think it was?"

Ben and Cindy shot each other a knowing look and smiled.

"Now if you kids will excuse me, I have to head over to your school. Heard there was a, uh, plumbing problem or something there last night," the sheriff said, uncomfortably.

"Plumbing problem?" Cindy asked.

"Yeah, yeah, a plumbing problem!" Sheriff Cyphers said, heading over to his police car. "They're gonna have to close the school for a couple of days to fix it. Big mess. I'm gonna go check it out, uh, now."

"Hey, nerd!" Don said. "Did you have anything to do this?" he asked, half-accusing, half-curious.

Ben and Cindy looked at each other again.

"Don, you wouldn't believe us if we told you," Ben said, and he and Cindy walked away from a very long night.

"Hey, nerd! Come back here!" Don called. "I'm not done talkin' to you. I'm not d – "

Don clammed right up as something in the air caught his eye. Something with a large wingspan. Something that resembled a huge flying lizard, flapping its wings against the receding glow of the moon. Don stood there, mouth hanging open, as he watched a real live monster fly off into the sky.

"Hey, Ben!" Don called. "Wait up! Can I see that monster book of yours? Hey, Ben, come on!"

Ben turned and waited. Don joined them.

"Maybe you know what you're talking about after all," Don said.

EPILOGUE

"I THOUGHT THE KIDS made a mess, but this is a million times worse," said the custodian to no one. After the events of last night – and who knew what happened, thanks to there being no security cameras – Kurtzberg Middle School was closed. There were two huge holes in the walls, the gym was trashed, the art room was a crazy mess . . . and there was only one custodian to deal with it all!

The custodian walked through the hallway, inspecting the row of open lockers and some enormous footprints that appeared burned into the floor. He sighed.

"It's gonna take more than floor wax to clean this up," he said.

As he walked past the lockers surveying the damage, something caught his eye.

There was something on the floor.

He knelt down and saw a little blob. He poked it with a finger.

The blob slowly oozed over the finger.

THE END?

MONSTERS UNLEASHED!

CULLEN BUNN -- *WRITER*
STEVE McNIVEN -- *PENCILER*
JAY LEISTEN -- *INKER*
DAVID CURIEL -- *COLOR ARTIST*
VC's TRAVIS LANHAM -- *LETTERER*

STEVE McNIVEN, WITH JAY LEISTEN & DAVID CURIEL
COVER ART

GEOF DARROW; FRANCESCO FRANCAVILLA; STEVE McNIVEN; KEN NIIMURA; MIKE MIGNOLA WITH DAVE STEWART
VARIANT COVERS

MIKE DEODATO, JR. WITH FRANK D'ARMATA
HIP-HOP VARIANT

JEE-HYUNG LEE
MARVEL FUTURE FIGHT VARIANT COVER

CHRISTINA HARRINGTON -- *ASSISTANT EDITOR*
MARK PANICCIA -- *EDITOR*

AXEL ALONSO	**JOE QUESADA**	**DAN BUCKLEY**	**ALAN FINE**
EDITOR IN CHIEF	*CHIEF CREATIVE OFFICER*	*PUBLISHER*	*EXECUTIVE PRODUCER*

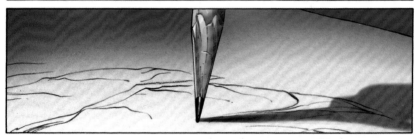

SHOOOOM

THE STORY CONTINUES IN THE MONSTERS UNLEASHED COMIC SERIES
Available in comic shops and on the Marvel Comics App.